SPARK

FEYLAND BOOK 4

ANTHEA SHARP

Fiddlehead Press

COPYRIGHT

PROLOGUE

THE DARK QUEEN of the Realm of Faerie paced over the moon-dappled mosses before her tangled throne. Her skirts flared out into gossamer shadows, and diamonds sparkled in her black hair like tiny, cold stars, capturing the light of the sickle moon high overhead. Every step she took snapped with frustration, and the creatures of her court flinched as the reverberations of their queen's anger echoed through the realm.

Even the powerful horned hunter and his red-eyed hounds stayed at the far edges of the clearing, the star-tarnished oaks at their backs. The court musicians stood in a huddled trio, fingers quiet upon their instruments. Only the fearful whispers of the denizens of the Dark Court sawed the edge off the silence.

The queen halted, the still before the storm, and the last whispers died. From the darkened pathway a figure made of shadows came; a knight bearing an enormous blade. He strode past the violet bonfire, the flames licking eerie reflections on his black armor; past the feral and nameless creatures of the court, past the hollow-eyed banshee, and the sharp-toothed goblins with their caps of blood.

"My lady." He went down on one knee and bowed his black-helmed head in supplication.

"What have you found?" Her voice was shaded with wrath.

"It is as you guessed. The opening between the mortal world and our own remains but a thin crack. Nothing has changed since that gateway was closed through deceitful mortal and fey means."

"Curse the Elder Fey!" She clenched her fists, and frost striated the velvet-deep mosses beneath her feet. "We are no more than beggars for the scraps of dreams, where once we were feared across every human land. There must be a way to enter the human world freely, and harvest the essence of our power."

"If there is, we will not discover that means in the realm, my lady."

The queen's eyes narrowed. "Then we must find someone who can. Surely there is one among the mortals who would bend to the needs of the realm."

She whirled, and the fey folk cowered from the sharpness of her smile.

"Scouts, keep watch on the faerie ring. Soon enough, a human will stumble into the Dark Realm—and when they do, we will be ready. This time, there will be no escape."

CHAPTER ONE

SPARK JAXLEY WAITED outside her temporary mansion, the fog of her breath matching the cold clouds overhead. A gleaming limousine grav-car hovered by the curb with her luggage packed inside, and her security guards were deployed strategically around the manicured lawn—far enough away to give her the illusion of space, but ready to spring into action if needed.

Not that she had anything to be worried about in the controlled compound of The View. No clamoring autograph-seekers or paparazzi trying to get a candid shot of the most famous sim gamer in the world. No lines of cars driving slowly past, no screaming fans gathered in front of the wrought-iron gates.

There was only a single bird flitting through the land-scaped shrubbery and the distant noise of the city below. Spark was glad of the solitude. This goodbye was going to be hard enough as it was.

The early spring air held a bite, the chill slipping past her scarf to touch her neck with icy fingers. Spark re-wound her scarf—magenta, to match her hair—then slid her hands into the fur-lined pockets of her jacket while she waited for her friends to arrive.

Friends—the last thing she'd expected to find when she came to Crestview. Stuck in an insignificant city for a month wasn't her idea of a prime trip. But VirtuMax paid her plenty to be their spokesmodel, and part of the contract included beta-testing their immersive new FullD equipment and its launch game, Feyland. Which meant coming to their exclusive compound in the center of exactly nowhere.

She never thought her life would change so completely as a result.

She sighed softly, and Burt, the head of her security team, glanced her way. "Would you prefer to wait inside, Miss Jaxley?"

"No, thanks."

She'd rather feel the weak sun on her face, breathe the fresh air. After all, she was about to be cooped up in various forms of transportation for the next seven hours. SimCon, her next destination, was half a continent away.

"Spark!"

A girl with long blond hair walked up the driveway, her arm around a tall, lean guy, their steps in perfect synch. Jennet Carter and Tam Linn. Spark tried to ignore the little spurt of envy heating her blood. Not that she wished they weren't together; they were perfect for each other. It was just—she wanted that, too. But with her crazy life, she didn't have the option to hook up with a guy in any meaningful way.

Besides, all the ones she met were blinded by her fame, or wanted to use it. Or weren't quite right for her. Like the one driving up in his fancy red grav-car.

Roy Lassiter. True, they'd shared some intense experiences, but no matter how hard she tried to fall for him, she couldn't manage it.

"Hey," Roy said, getting out his car and giving her his super-charming smile. For once, it looked real.

Spark smiled back, wishing she knew what to say. She could tell Roy was hoping for something: a secret love note, her private number, a promise she couldn't give. Jennet and Tam's arrival saved her, and she turned to them, glad for the distraction of Jennet's hug.

"I can't believe you have to leave," Jennet said. "Can't you stay a bit longer?"

"VirtuMax needs me at SimCon to debut the FullD," Spark said.

"Off to be a superstar, is it? Shake the lowly dust of Crestview off your shoes?" Roy squeezed her shoulders and was smart enough to let her go.

"I'm going to miss you guys," Spark said.

Tam nodded. "We'll stay in touch. After all…"

He glanced at the nearby security guard. Burt seemed out of earshot, but Tam was a careful guy. None of them wanted to broadcast the fact that they'd been deputized by magical beings to guard the mortal world. People would think they were insane. Or even worse, believe them. Faerie magic was power, and not many people could be trusted with it.

The whole thing seemed like a crazy sort of dream, except that seven of them had experienced the same thing. Eight if you counted Tam's friend Marny, who had dealt with the reality of the fey folk in her own way.

"Is Zeg coming?" Spark asked.

She wanted to say goodbye to the big guy. Even though he was old enough to be her dad, he was a gamer first. Like the rest of them, he'd fought in the final battle alongside the Elder Fey to keep the Realm of Faerie from rampaging through the human world.

"Yeah." Tam cocked his head. "I think I hear his car now."

Zeg's old gas-guzzler was as out of place in The View as a fly on vanilla ice cream, and he was proud of the fact. He took immense pleasure in using his official gate pass, and Spark suspected he deliberately messed with his car's engine before he drove up to the compound, making the car smoke and rattle even more than usual.

Sure enough, the coughing clatter coming up the street was unmistakable. Roy made a face, though he didn't say anything as Zeg's car rounded the corner and chugged up the drive. The guzzler halted with a squeal of brakes, and Zeg hopped out, his smile beaming from behind his frizzy beard. He had a passenger, too—his niece, Marny.

"Marny!" Jennet gave her friend a hug, her slight form dwarfed by the bigger girl. Marny was solid, physically as well as emotionally.

"Good to see you two," Spark said. "The gang's almost all here. Jennet, is your dad coming?"

"He's stuck at work, but sends his best wishes and an open invitation to come stay with us. You know, whenever you're passing through on your international tours."

They all laughed. Crestview wasn't on the way to anywhere.

"I might, actually. Now that VirtuMax owns this town, I imagine they'll want me back from time to time."

"Good," Roy said, a little too smugly. "There are other reasons to come back here, of course."

Spark caught Jennet's eye. Although he'd matured some, Roy Lassiter could still be a prime ego-head.

"Right," Marny said. "And I hate to tell you this, Roy, but you're not anywhere near the top of the list."

Tam let out a snort, and Jennet held up one hand.

"Stop it," she said. "Is this really how we want to say goodbye to Spark?"

"Just like old times." A hint of a smile tugged at Tam's mouth. "Think of all those happy in-game memories."

"Right." Spark rolled her eyes. "Especially the parts where we almost got killed."

"We'll talk, though," Jennet said. "We all have each other's messager numbers, right?"

"We have to." Tam's voice grew serious. "Feyland launches next week, which means our work is just starting. We need to be on the lookout for… you know. Freaky things."

Jennet nodded, and Marny crossed her arms. Spark let out a low breath. Yeah, they knew. Things like fey magic seeping out of the game into the mortal world. Gamers led astray, stumbling into a realm of wonder and trouble far beyond anything they'd imagined when they entered the virtual reality of a sim game.

"I'm sure we'll all keep watch," Zeg said. He handed Spark a paper sack. "Here. I baked you some cookies."

ANTHEA SHARP

That, more than anything, made sorrow tighten her throat. Zeg's cookies were legendary.

"Miss Jaxley," Burt called. "We need to get you to the airport."

Jennet, her blue eyes glinting with tears, hugged Spark again. Tam was next, then Marny, who nearly cracked her ribs. Zeg gave her a bear hug, and for a second Spark missed her dad, missed her whole family with a quick, sharp pain.

Still, she knew her family was happy for the opportunities and the life she'd chosen. Not to mention the big portion of her earnings she always sent home.

"Spark. I'll miss you." Roy put his arms around her, and it was too tender, too close to the real thing.

But *almost* wasn't enough. Regret surged through her, bittersweet.

"Bye, Roy," she said softly.

He bent to kiss her, and at the last second she turned her face so that his lips grazed her cheek, not her mouth.

Trying to ignore the hurt in his eyes, she stepped back and made herself smile. At the curb, Burt opened the limo door and cleared his throat.

"Stay out of trouble, team," she said.

Then, before she made a total spectacle of herself, she ducked into the car. Burt closed the door behind her, and the tinted glass hid the tissue she used to blot her tears. Internationally famous gaming stars didn't cry.

Much.

Aran Cole slid on the fake glasses with the dark frames, and turned to face his friend, Bix Chowney. The flickering fluorescent light in Bix's old garage cast a sickly glow over everything, but Aran was fond of the place; lumpy couch, faint mildew smell, and all.

It was the closest thing he had to a home. All he needed was a place to sleep, a hotplate, and power for his sim-system. The Viper was installed in the corner, hidden under a tarp when he wasn't gaming.

"How do I look?" he asked.

Bix tilted his head, the light giving his blond hair a greenish cast. "Boring, and respectable. That's freaky, man. How'd you do that?"

"It's all in the attitude. I just imagine I'm a geeklet from a nice, suburban family, and presto! No more slacker gamer."

He'd also re-dyed his hair to its underlying black, removing the blue streak, and had changed into the one button-down shirt he owned. His other shirts were all logo tees featuring obscure bands or gamer jokes, and he needed to project a more upper-class persona. At least until he passed through SimCon's registration.

"You making fun of me?" Bix punched his shoulder, hard enough to make it count.

"Hey—not my fault you're all well-adjusted and middle class. But you're not a geeklet."

Bix wanted to be edgy, but befriending Aran was the nearest he got. Not that Aran would recommend his particular lifestyle. Even Bix didn't know about Aran's other existence as the prime hacker known as BlackWing. He could find the exploits in any game, slipping in between the cracks in the code. Sadly, selling game hacks on the gray market wasn't making him rich. In fact, it was barely enough to survive on.

He needed enough cash to get his own apartment instead of couching it at Bix's and living off high-jolt soda and packaged ramen.

Aran's folks would feed him, grudgingly. Even though he was eighteen now, he still had a room at home. It stayed empty, though—just a place to store his stuff. That house held too much history and not enough forgiveness. Not even close. Unsaid words piled up like knives until he felt he was being sliced alive by their sharp edges.

He swigged the last of his super-caffeinated drink. The carbonation stung his throat and nose, but he needed the boost. It was way too early for him to be awake.

"Let's go," he said, grabbing his bag, a brown messenger pouch he'd liberated from his older brother.

Bix followed him out of the garage, carefully locking up. Aran had an extra key, though he'd resorted to climbing through the back window a couple times to keep Bix's parents from seeing him. He didn't think the Chowneys would approve of Aran squatting in their old garage. Not that they ever used it, with the fancy new construction they'd built out front to house their grav-cars.

The metro stop was six blocks away. Aran hunched his shoulders against the February drizzle and let Bix babble on about how excited he was to go to SimCon. It was the first time their city had hosted the gaming convention, and the nerds and geeks were completely turbo.

"Can you believe VirtuMax is *finally* unveiling the FullD system?" Bix's voice rose with enthusiasm. "It's been years since they announced the project. I hope it's as prime as they claim."

"Me too."

Despite the nonchalance he projected, Aran was excited—though not for the same reasons. He was burning to see VirtuMax unveil their long-delayed FullD system and try the immersive new game that came with it: Feyland. If he could get a head-start on cracking the programming, he'd be set. Make enough cash to move someplace where the sun actually shone in the winter.

Maybe he'd buy one of those old-style camping vans, figure out a way to install his gaming systems, and travel around, following the warmth and the cons.

But first, he had a game to hack.

"Spark Jaxley will be at the debut." Bix grinned. "I hope we can get close enough to touch her."

Practically every gamer in the world was in love with the celebrity simmer—guys and girls alike. She was cute, sure, but Aran would bet that most people never realized—the way he, as a true hacker, did—that her gaming skills were flawless.

Which probably meant she was a class A diva.

"You can ask her out," Aran said as they headed down the dingy steps of the subway station. "Guy like you, how could she refuse?"

"Shut it," Bix said. "At least we'll get to see her play."

In the stink and whoosh of the tunnels, Bix passed his wrist, with its embedded chip, over the gate scanner. Aran dumped a handful of grubby coins into the machine. If Bix weren't with him, he would have jumped the gate, but he was playing it straight today. No thrill of eluding the security guys and dashing onto the train at the last second.

It was a quiet ride down to the convention center, though the train filled the closer they got. Half the passengers were dressed for a day at the office. The rest were obviously on their way to SimCon, flaunting their gamer garb and inner freaks. Aran concentrated on relaxing, sinking deeper into his character of regular-gamer-geek.

"Do you think the plan will work?" Bix asked as the train pulled into the downtown station.

"Of course." Aran hoped.

They went along with the flow of people headed out of the station and toward the gleaming glass and steel complex housing the convention center. Once inside the main building, they were hit with the smell of industrial carpet and the babble of excited fans.

"Volunteers, over there." Bix pointed at the sign, then cut across the crowd.

Aran followed, rubbing his thumb over the chip glued on the inside of his wrist. As long as no one took a close look, he'd pass.

"Slow down," he said, tapping Bix's shoulder.

"Sorry."

Bix fell back, fidgeting with the edge of his coat. They joined the queue at the volunteer check-in table, and Aran pushed his friend ahead. Best to let the genuine guy go first. The lady in front of them was wearing sparkly wings. She had to take them off and let the security guard on duty inspect them to prove they weren't wired as transmitters or something. Finally approved, she grabbed her badge with a loud snort of annoyance and stomped off, wings glittering.

Aran swallowed, his throat suddenly dry, and nudged Bix forward. Show time.

CHAPTER TWO

Aran made himself breathe regularly, despite the sudden speeding of his heartbeat. It wasn't as if he'd get arrested if this didn't work—but he'd certainly be kicked to the curb. He didn't have the cash for a ticket, and he wouldn't pass any kind of background check. This was his only chance to get into SimCon.

The man at the volunteer check-in table was thin and pale, with a silver stud piercing his left eyebrow. He looked up at Bix with a disinterested expression.

"Name?"

"Bix Chowney. And my friend, Aran Cole."

"Scan."

Bix passed his wrist over the scanner, which chirped acknowledgement. The man at the table flipped through his alphabetized box, then handed Bix his volunteer badge. It was attached to a bright red lanyard with *VirtuMax* printed up and down the entire length, leaving no doubt about who was the biggest sponsor at SimCon.

"Here's your registration packet. Gofer Central is down the hall. Next."

With what he hoped was a casual expression, Aran passed his wrist over the scanner. The machine remained silent.

"Not again," Aran said, putting frustration behind the words. "That's the third time this week."

He made a show of pulling back his cuff and inspecting his wrist, letting the man at the table see the glint of the chip.

"Seriously?" Bix said. "I thought you had that replaced."

He hit the right blend of exasperation and nerves, and Aran swallowed back a smile.

"Yeah, well, my mom's been too busy." Aran waved his arm over the scanner again, with the same lack of result.

"Spell your last name," the man said in a bored voice.

Aran did, and kept himself from looking at Bix in triumph when the man gave him his badge and packet.

"Keep your badge visible at all times," the man told them. "Both of you, head to Gofer Central. Down that hall, second door on the left. Next." He looked past them, their names and features already forgotten.

Turning away from the table, Aran let a grin cross his face. That had gone more smoothly than he'd hoped.

"We did it! We got you in." Bix was smiling like a fool.

"You were good back there," Aran said. "Ever think of becoming an actor?"

"Not with pros like you showing how it's done. I never would have guessed that was a fake ch—"

"Hey, don't shout it to the whole con."

Not that wearing a fake wrist-chip was illegal. People who couldn't afford the real thing sometimes put on dud chips for show, but duping the authorities by pretending to be legitimate was a road to trouble. The longer Aran could avoid official notice, the better.

He had his badge now, which would give him access to almost everywhere in the conference. Gofers were the lowest level of con volunteer, and as a result nobody looked at them too closely.

Which was exactly how he wanted it.

Gofer Central was impossible to miss. The big hand-lettered sign was their first clue, along with the volunteers darting in and out of the room. Just inside the door stood a dark-haired girl wearing glasses and holding a tablet. Her badge read *Matila—VC*.

"Hi," she said when Aran and Bix stepped over the threshold. "I'm Matila, the volunteer coordinator. Badges, please."

They held them up and she scanned them with her tablet. A check mark appeared by their names.

"Welcome to SimCon, guys. Ever volunteered at a gaming convention before?"

"Nope," Aran said, while Bix shook his head.

"Okay," she said. "Check your packets—you'll have specific duties assigned, based on the questionnaire you filled out when you applied to volunteer. Since this is the first time for both of you, the jobs will probably be boring, but hey, they're a necessary part of keeping the con running. You're expected to put your hours in every day. Other than that, have fun, try to get some sleep, and don't forget to shower now and then."

"Do we get shirts?" Bix asked.

"Over there." The coordinator waved at a long table at one side of the room. "If you need anything else, let me know."

"Thanks," Aran said, as he and Bix headed into the controlled chaos of Gofer Central.

A dozen volunteers flurried through the room, all wearing the black and silver SimCon shirt, with *volunteer* blazoned across the back.

On the opposite side from the T-shirts, another long table held snacks and drinks, primarily of the salty, sugary, fatty, and caffeinated variety. The bulletin board beside it was plastered with signs and flyers and notes pertaining to every aspect of SimCon.

"Shirts first," Aran said, steering them over to the table.

A blue-haired girl found their sizes and checked them off her list. "You can change in the bathroom next door," she said, then winked at Aran. "Or right here in front of me. I don't mind."

Bix cleared his throat, and Aran jabbed him in the side with his elbow.

"Come on," Aran said. "Two seconds of showing your manly chest isn't going to scar you for life."

"It might scar me, though," a nearby volunteer called.

"Close your eyes, weenie," the T-shirt girl said.

While she was distracted, Bix whipped off his shirt and donned the SimCon tee. Aran unbuttoned his "geeklet" shirt, aware he was gathering a few appreciative stares. For half a second he considered going into the other room, but it seemed a foolish waste of time. He was in good shape; not that he was planning to make a strip show of himself. With quick, efficient motions he changed, then bowed at the smattering of applause.

"Show off," Bix said, with no hint of jealousy. "You have too many muscles. I should steal back that kung-fu game."

"Like you ever played it." Aran pulled his schedule out of his packet. "Where are you assigned?"

It would be a problem if he and Bix were working the same area, but otherwise he'd be able to finesse his way through. His most important goal here was to get as close as possible to a FullD system, and he was confident he would. Sometimes hacking life was easier than cracking game code.

Bix glanced at his schedule. "I'm checking badges at the main exhibition hall. You?"

"Doing set up in the theater," Aran said.

His real assignment was helping calibrate projectors in the presentation rooms. He'd hit the theater first, then come up with some plausible excuse when he showed up late for his actual job.

"Sweet! Maybe you'll see Spark Jaxley. Wanna trade?"

"I doubt I'll see her. And you get to check out where all the best swag is in the Expo Hall. See you back here in two hours."

"Right." Bix tipped up his chin in farewell and went out the door.

Aran folded his map of the convention center and stuck it in his back pocket. He had the place memorized, down to the stairwells and fire exits. Even the janitorial closets. It was always good to know where to go for extra cover. He headed down the corridors to the theater, practicing his "I'm completely official here" stride.

A beefy security guard stood in front of the main theater doors, arms folded. Aran flashed his badge and papers at the man. "Tech support."

Without a word, the guard let him in.

The theater smelled of anticipation, and a blend of hairspray and scorched dust from the hot stage lights. The house was dim, the stage illuminated by a spotlight and a screen glowing with the VirtuMax logo in silver and red. Aran paused behind the rows of empty seats and watched as three guys carried a FullD system to the center of the stage.

"Pull the spot a little more left," a man at the front of the theater called. "Get that rig up front, guys."

The beam hit the gaming system and it shone, chrome details and polished magenta fittings sparking under the spotlight. The sim chair seat was cushioned in black synth-leather, and even the cables leading out from the system looked high end; thick and substantial, in straight lines instead of the usual noodle of cords.

Time for him to get to work. Hovering too long in the shadows would make him look suspicious. Aran strode down the aisle, heading for the man he guessed was the stage manager.

"Hey," he said. "They sent me to help with tech set-up."

The man squinted at his badge. "Aran, is it? Know your way around sim equip?"

"Oh yeah. I've rebuilt and upgraded my Viper a dozen times."

His system was fully overclocked at this point, modded into a machine capable of things the designers had never planned for. He'd put too many hours and too much cash into the system, but it had been worth it.

Now, though, the imminent release of the FullD changed everything. Bix would let him use the system he'd pre-ordered

—and there were always the sim-cafes—but Aran couldn't afford to wait until official launch day to start playing.

Having SimCon here, in his own town, made it easier to get the jump on finding the inevitable hacks and exploits in the programming. Whoever was first to market with the Feyland cheats would make a pile of money. Aran intended to be that person.

After that, well, he'd like to go clean. He'd wash the hacker slime off, brush up his honest gaming skills, and maybe even get good enough for the tournament circuit.

"Right," the stage manager said. "Talk to PJ over there—he'll put you to work."

Five minutes later, Aran was taping wires to the floor with black gaffer's tape. He started back at the VGA/mixing board, shadowed in the wings. On hands and knees, he worked his way up to the gleaming sim-system. Sort of like a worshipper approaching a shrine, which was both true and ironic.

The rip of tape blended with the other sounds of set-up, oddly relaxing despite the jangle in his blood. This close to the system, he smelled the newness of it—fresh plas-metal and enamel paint, and all tempting. He laid the last piece of tape, then stood.

Damn, he wanted to try it out. Slowly, he ran his palm over the soft synth-leather of the chair. Envy coiled in the pit of his stomach, spiced with fierce yearning.

"Nice, isn't it?" a clear, female voice said.

Aran jerked his hand back as if he'd been caught snitching candy. He looked up to see the famous, magenta-haired figure of Spark Jaxley striding onto stage. She was geared up in a suit straight from one of the sim games: molded and shiny, and showing off her curves.

Aran's mouth went dry, and he was glad of his mixed heritage, the dusky skin that hid the flush he felt warming his cheeks. He'd laughed at Bix's fanboy moments, but standing there, with the real live Spark Jaxley in front of him, Aran had to admit he understood the attraction.

Spark didn't drop her smile, though a possessive jolt ran through her at the sight of the guy standing next to her FullD.

"Ah, yeah," he said. "This is the first model I've seen in person. It's prime."

She kept walking, coming right into his personal space, close enough to read his badge. He didn't back off, just gave her a half smile in return. His eyes were slightly tilted, as if one of his parents was Asian, and he was good looking, despite the clunky black glasses obscuring half his face.

"I can't wait to see you play," he said.

There was the usual admiration in his voice—she was tired of being adored by people who didn't even know her—but there was sincerity, too. He really did want to see her show off the system.

"You're a simmer." She didn't need to make it a question.

It was obvious in the way the guy (Aran, according to his badge) had been looking at the FullD. She felt that same pull herself; the lure of immersing herself in a fabulous world, of testing her formidable skills and beating anything the programmers could dream up.

Although the Realm of Faerie was a whole other challenge. Luckily, only a few gamers would ever stumble into that world. When they did, she and the rest of the Feyguard would be there to pull them back out.

"I sim," Aran said. "Hey, could I get your autograph?"

"Of course. Got a pen?"

He fished around in his jeans pockets, coming up with a folded map of the convention center and a pen with the VirtuMax logo printed on the side.

"Thanks," he said, handing them to her. "Make it out to Bix. B-I-X."

"Your name isn't Aran?" She shot another look at his badge.

"It's for a friend. He's a big fan."

"I'll be in the VirtuMax area tomorrow. He could meet me then." She wrote out the name and signed her autograph, then handed the pen and paper back to Aran.

"Maybe. But he's shy—and there'll be about a thousand other people who'll want your autograph. This way, your hand will be spared from signing one more."

She laughed a little. "I like your logic. You know, there'll be demo models of the FullD for people to try."

"I know." His dark brown eyes sparked with interest. "Although there's still that problem of the thousand other people."

She tilted her head and studied him a moment. There was something appealing about this guy, beyond the fact he wasn't a complete mess of fannish drool at her feet. And he was cute. *Rebounding from your almost-crush on Roy?* a voice inside her

SPARK

needled. But there was no such thing as a not-falling-in-love rebound.

"Listen," she said. "You've got a badge. Come in early tomorrow. I'll clear you with security, and make sure you get some system time. Say, around nine? Con opens at ten."

He gave her a surprised look, quickly overtaken by a grin. "That'd be great."

"Miss Jaxley," the stage manager called. "All done with your little meet-n-greet up there? We need to check the feed to the screens."

"See you tomorrow," she said. "Nice meeting you, Aran."

"You too, Miss Jax—"

"Call me Spark. Not nearly enough people do."

His smile emphasized his high cheekbones. "All right, Spark. Later."

The stage manager cleared his throat. Aran tucked the paper and pen in his back pocket, then jumped down off the stage, lean and agile.

"Miss Jaxley," the tech said, "here's your gear."

Spark took the gleaming helm and visor and pulled on the LED-studded gaming gloves. Just before she slid into the sim chair to begin running the interface, she saw Aran in the back of the theater. He lifted his hand in farewell, then slipped out, leaving only shadows behind.

CHAPTER THREE

"NO WAY!" Bix snatched the folded paper with Spark's autograph out of Aran's fingers and pressed it theatrically over his heart. "Now I really hate you, man."

"Give that back." Aran held out his hand. "I'm sure someone around here would show a little appreciation for a custom autograph."

"Seriously—I owe you," Bix said.

"Not really." Aran shifted his weight to the balls of his feet, then back to his heels. "I didn't get much opportunity to talk to Spark. Hey—any chance you can show up to the con early tomorrow?"

Bix's frown scrunched up his forehead. "The only way I can come at *all* tomorrow is if I go to worship with my family in the morning. They're practically foaming at the mouth at the thought of me spending any time here on the Sabbath."

"Among the unwashed heathens and devil gamers, right? At least you can still attend."

For once, Aran was glad of Bix's hyper-religious parents. If

Bix had been able to come, Aran would have found a way to finagle him time on the new FullD systems—but this way, Aran didn't have to ask Spark's forgiveness for bringing along an uninvited guest.

Not that he was telling Bix exactly where he'd be at nine a.m. Getting the autograph almost erased the guilt he felt at not revealing that Spark Jaxley had invited him to come early and try out the FullD.

Not only would Bix be beyond jealous, Aran didn't want his friend to know—or even guess at—what he did to make a living. Sim hackers were not universally loved. Pretty much the opposite, in fact.

Sure, everybody wanted to know the cheats and exploits, but it was a sneaky, underhanded way to turn a profit. The honorable players refused to use the hacks, and then were at a disadvantage because of their nobleness. Bix was one of those, and he'd said dozens of times how much he despised the scum that found the exploits in the first place and then sold the information. If he saw Aran playing an advance version of the game, and then BlackWing started selling hacks before the system was released—well, Bix wasn't dumb.

"Come on," Bix said. "There's a new combat game demo at one of the booths, and they're raffling off good stuff to try and get attention. Even a new Slix system."

"An almost obsolete sim set-up. Just what every gamer needs."

"Not everybody is going to be moving to the FullD when it releases next week. And maybe VirtuMax's design is still full of bugs. They took long enough to launch the thing. Come on."

Aran followed his friend through the increasingly crowded floor of the Expo Hall. Posters featuring Spark Jaxley kept catching his eye, especially that particular shade of magenta hair nobody could quite match. Plenty of gamers, both male and female, tried. One in ten people at the convention had some variation of pinkish-reddish hair.

But none of them were Spark.

Tomorrow, he reminded himself.

"Five minutes, Miss Jaxley," the stage manager said.

Spark nodded from her position in the wings. For a few more minutes she could be just herself, a nervous seventeen-year-old standing in the shadows. The moment she stepped out under the lights, she'd be the sim queen, the celebrated gamer, the girl people loved, envied, and hated in equal measure.

In the early months of her fame, she'd read all her fan mail herself. Until the day she got the death threat, complete with gruesome details. It had shaken her. Not the gory descriptions, but that someone out there in the world loathed her so much they'd send all that negativity her way.

She probably still got horrible messages, but she had a secretary now who screened everything, only forwarding the real fan mail for her to answer.

On stage, the emcee began the VirtuMax introduction, talking about the search for a seamless virtual experience, the incredible talent who worked on the project, and the faerie-world inspiration behind Feyland.

If only they knew.

The game had connected to the actual Realm of Faerie in ways she didn't quite understand. The lead programmer, a guy named Thomas Rimer, had drawn on old faerie lore and legends to create the content. And then, somehow, the realm had crossed over into reality. Tam and Jennet had tried to explain, but at a certain point there were no answers beyond one.

Magic.

"And now," the emcee announced, "as part of an exclusive SimCon demo, please help me welcome Spark Jaxley!"

The crowd cheered, the noise raw and excited. A stagehand pressed a wireless mic into her palm, and Spark stepped onto the stage. The noise redoubled, and she let it wash over her. She couldn't see faces beyond the blare of the lights, but she smiled as if she could.

"Hey, everybody," she said into the mic. "It's good to be here."

She waited as the audience settled down. Not too far down, though; the theater still buzzed with a low hum of excitement. The premiere of the FullD system was the whole point of SimCon, after all.

She strode over to where the gleaming system sat, spot-lit in the center of the stage.

"Here it is," she said. "The sim-system we've been waiting years for. VirtuMax's FullD!"

More shouts and applause. She grinned at the invisible crowd.

"Want me to fire it up?" The noise rose in volume—but not enough. "Are you sure?"

The theater practically shook. Spark lowered her mic and swept her gaze across the barely visible packed seats, nodding. At last the frenzy subsided.

"I'll give you a taste tonight of what the system can do, and show you highlights of Feyland. Tomorrow morning we'll have a number of FullD systems on the floor for you all to try out."

Not enough, of course, and the lines would be severely long. At least some of the convention-goers would get a chance to play. The ones that didn't would just have to be content with an autographed picture.

Spark handed her mic to the emcee, then pulled on the gaming helm they'd wired into the theater display system. Even though the watching crowd wouldn't be able to feel what she felt, they'd see and hear her gameplay; plus she'd do her best to narrate everything she was experiencing in-game.

She settled into the chair and loaded up the character creation screen of Feyland.

"Most of you are familiar with the types of characters here," she said. "We've got casters, distance fighters, healers, melee classes—but a few new twists, too."

With a couple of quick finger commands she called up her avatar, a magenta-haired character with pointed ears and a bow strapped to her back.

"This is the avatar I played in beta. She's a Kitsune, with control over the elements and a few surprise talents." Spark sent her character into Feyland, where she materialized in the familiar ring of mushrooms. "As you see, when you first enter the game, you're in a clearing in the woods, surrounded by a faerie ring."

She paused a moment, concentrating on the sensations.

"There's a breeze—I can feel it against my cheeks. The moss underfoot is soft and springy, like walking on crash-test foam."

That got a small laugh. Smiling, Spark stepped over the ring—pale mushrooms mixed with white-dotted red ones—and gestured to the path leading between the trees. "Following that path takes you to your first adventure. I'll let you explore that part yourselves. No point in ruining *all* the surprises. For now, we'll jump ahead to the city."

She keyed in the command to take her to the next preset scene. After a quick fade to black, her character reappeared on the crest of a hill overlooking a city. White towers gleamed, colorful pennants flying over an orderly maze of cobbled streets. A high wall enclosed the buildings, and the glint of a lake at the far side of the city was just visible, the blue waters shining beneath the sun.

"The city of Stronghold," she said. "Here you'll find vendors, combat trainers, and a huge variety of quests that send you off to explore the many fantastical areas of Feyland."

Though, hopefully, not to the Dark Court, where the merciless and lovely queen ruled, hungry for entry into the mortal world. Spark shivered at the memory of the queen's sharp-edged smile. Quickly, she sent her character striding down the road and through the city gates.

Non-player characters, NPCs, thronged the streets, selling their wares: bunches of herbs and flowers, loaves of bread, shiny knives. One corner boasted a juggler, while another featured a yellow-haired girl playing the fiddle. Sounds and smells filled the air, and Spark did her best to describe the mix of fresh-baked bread, dust, and lavender.

"We'll swing by the Lucky Tavern," she said, cutting through an alleyway. "Always good to start your questing with a refreshing beverage."

The crowd laughed at that, as they were supposed to.

Spark entered the tavern and ordered a tankard of ale. She took a swig, then set it with a clunk on the wooden bar.

"Doesn't taste too bad, though nothing like real ale. Not that I'd know, being below the drinking age." She made her character wink, and the crowd joined in her amusement. "I heard that in the early stages of development, everything in-game tasted like bananas. Compared to that, ale is divine. You can order fruit juice or water, too, if that's more your speed. VirtuMax tries to cover all the bases—though I've yet to see an espresso stand in the city."

"Maybe someone should start one up!" a guy called from the crowd.

"He'd get business," Spark said. "Actually, one of the upcoming expansions includes an interactive life simulation, so if your dream is to become a shopkeeper in Stronghold, with a few adventures on the side, you can do that. Or you can just spend all your time killing monsters. Speaking of which…"

She activated the final demo sequence. Her character materialized at the edge of a lake. Sunlight sparkled off the silver-blue water, and behind her stretched a field of golden grain. In front of her, though, the earth was charred and barren, a blackened swath leading up to a tumbled pile of boulders that were obviously the lair of some dire creature.

"One of the interesting things about Feyland," she said, sending her character toward the stones, "is that the fights change, depending on your characters and party members. If I were in a group with a heavily armored fighter and a caster, for example, I'd find a different monster waiting ahead. As it is, the fights are challenging, though not impossible."

Unless the gamer stumbled into the Realm of Faerie. But her job was to make sure that didn't happen.

"So, you're on easy mode?" some heckler called.

"No. I might die in this fight, which would be embarrassing." The crowd chuckled along with her. "Just like in other games, dying is pretty inconvenient, and involves corpse-running. That is, taking time to run your ghost from the graveyard back to where you died, so you can reincorporate."

She strode up to the very edge of the rocks and drew her bow from her back. Then, cautiously, she crept forward. Past the first outcropping lay an open area of bare ground, and behind it gaped the dark maw of a cave.

"It smells bad here—like charred hair and rotten meat. The developers had fun with the scent-scapes, though not everything is nasty in-game. I should have mentioned that the tavern smelled like wood smoke and baking bread."

Something stirred in the back of the cave, and adrenaline spun through her. Quickly, she nocked an arrow and ducked for the partial cover of the granite boulder beside her.

With a scuttling rush, a creature charged into the clearing. Half lizard, half fighting rooster, it had the sharp-beaked head and nasty talons of a bird and a long, whip-like tail ending in a wicked spike. The whole hideous package stood over ten feet tall. It scanned the clearing and let out an angry shriek.

"Basilisk," she said in a low voice. "Paralyzes for two seconds with its gaze, highly venomous bite, lethal tail spike."

Spark's focus tightened until she forgot she was in a demo game. The watching crowd faded until there was nothing but her character, and the fight.

Aiming for one of the creature's yellow-crusted eyes, Spark let her arrow fly, then ducked back behind her boulder. The basilisk let out a squawk that sounded more annoyed than pain-filled. Damn, she'd missed. Which meant she now had a fully pissed-off bird looking to kill her.

She bent low and ran to a smaller tumble of rocks. Barely in time. The spike of the creature's tail stabbed through the air where she'd just been. It was hard for her to take aim at the basilisk while avoiding its line of sight. She shot another arrow, this one landing in the joint of the creature's leg.

Unfortunately, its lizard scales plated the basilisk in nearly impenetrable armor. She had to find its weak spots. There might be one behind its ankle, though with that sharp spur it wasn't an easy target. Better than the eyes, though, which were going to be hard to reach unless she got a perfect shot.

A drop of venom splashed from the basilisk's mouth, scorching the ground and sending up a waft of toxic smoke.

Spark tucked and rolled, coming up under the creature's belly. Drawing her boot dagger, she slashed at the back of its ankle, above where the sharp spur jutted out. The blade slid harmlessly off the thick scales, and she had to fling herself to the side as the basilisk hissed and kicked out.

Okay, not vulnerable in the ankle.

Breath rasping in her throat, Spark darted back toward the cover of the rocks. A painful heat hit the back of her shoulders, and her steps slowed until she stood motionless, facing the solid granite, but not protected by it. The basilisk had caught her in its evil gaze.

Come on—move! She desperately tried to budge, but her character was frozen, helpless. Her heartbeat pulsed through her, quick and urgent. She could hear the basilisk approaching behind her, its steps unhurried. It knew it had her.

Except... it didn't.

Spark called up her trump card, and the reason she'd picked a Kitsune to play in the first place. The scene in front of her shifted, the colors washing out, the sounds three times louder. She was dimly aware of the audience reaction as she morphed into fox form.

The basilisk was nearly upon her. She heard it halt and bend down, the snick of its beak opening as it prepared to give its venomous death bite.

Whirling, she gathered her four paws under her and leaped.

She landed on the back of the basilisk's neck, where scales turned to feathers. Scrabbling for purchase, she forced herself closer to the top of its head. The creature shrieked and shook, trying to dislodge her. Droplets of burning venom singed her fur. She was slipping...

And then she was holding on, back in her human form, her dagger still in her hand. She raised it high and plunged it into the basilisk's right eye. The blade entered with a liquid splat and the creature swayed.

Spark leaped free as the basilisk toppled to the ground, dead. Her heartbeat sounded loud in her ears, but the familiar victory rush sang through her blood—fear turning to exhilaration in that curious, quicksilver alchemy she loved.

The watching crowd cheered, and Spark blinked herself back to reality. She wiped the sticky blade of her dagger and re-sheathed it, then pumped one fist high. The applause rose.

"There you have it," she said. "A taste of Feyland. Did you like it?"

The audience responded with screams of approval as she logged out of the game and pulled off her helmet.

A strand of her hair was stuck to her cheek and she felt a trickle of perspiration drip down her neck. It was hot under the lights, and she was flushed with success. A tech handed her a bottle of water. She took a quick gulp, then strode to the front of the stage.

The watching faces were still smudges, and she wondered for a second where Aran was in the crowd.

"I don't need to remind you to come early tomorrow," she said. "The demo line will be long, and I'm sorry that not everyone will get a chance at the FullD. As a consolation, I'll be at the VirtuMax booth signing autographs. Please stop by."

"I'll take your consolation any day!" a guy yelled, and the crowd laughed in agreement.

Spark smiled, but didn't respond. She'd learned not to engage. Last year, she'd had a brief interplay with someone in the crowd who had then ended up stalking her for months. Not fun.

Pulsing music rose through the speakers and the lights flashed through the spectrum of colors. The show was over. Waving, she sent her gaze across the entire theater, then headed for the wings.

The soft shadows enfolded her, and Spark drew in a breath. That had been some good play, though half the crowd wouldn't believe it hadn't been scripted beforehand. She didn't do well with scripts.

In the early days, VirtuMax had tried to run her through pre-planned scenarios. She'd hated them, and finally had insisted on playing live. It gave her the edge she needed, knowing that she could fail in front of everyone. And she had failed a couple of times—which just seemed to endear her even more to her fans.

"Great job, Miss Jaxley," the emcee said, coming up and slapping her on the shoulder. "You going to any of the parties?"

"Not tonight. Big day tomorrow."

She needed a shower, and some rest. Besides, the parties got old fast. It wasn't her idea of a fun time, being surrounded by people who either were too tongue-tied to say anything or were doing their best to impress her, and making fools out of themselves in the process. None of it was genuine.

Longing for her friends in Crestview twisted through her. When she got back to her suite, she'd message Jennet and they could share some girl gossip. Maybe she'd even tell Jennet about meeting a cute guy today.

Spark smiled wryly at the thought. Everyone assumed being a star must be wonderful, but she was grateful for any bit of normalcy she could find in her crazy life.

CHAPTER FOUR

C<small>LUTCHING HIS LARGE SODA</small>—<small>HIS</small> second of the morning—
Aran showed his badge to the convention center guard in the
booth.

"Aran Cole," he said. "Early appointment with VirtuMax."

He hoped Spark hadn't forgotten to put him on the list.

Apparently she hadn't, because the guard nodded and
buzzed him into the eerily quiet convention center. Eight
hours ago, the place had been humming with late-night
energy and side parties. He and Bix, by virtue of their badges
and official volunteer T-shirts, had been able to attend a fair
number of gatherings.

At some point during the evening a woman dressed as a
robo-enforcer, and her friend, a scantily clad warrior princess
with a tongue as sharp as her blade, had hooked up with them.
They'd danced to old-school club music; heavy, bone-shaking
beats that made the masked and be-sparkled creatures on the
temporary dance floor seem as though they were all one big

creature. A huge organism, with each fan comprising an individual cell.

Aran had tried a cup of weirdly-glowing blue punch, and hadn't even finished it. He wasn't much of a drinker, plus he wanted to be sharp the next morning. Bix got a little wilder, and Aran had to talk him out of going home with the robo-enforcer. As it was, they'd barely made the last train to Bix's neighborhood. Aran had given him a boost through his bedroom window, then crawled into his own nest in the lightless back garage.

Now, Aran felt himself waking up as he walked between the still booths, making for the section marked off by VirtuMax. That part of the Expo Hall was anything but sleepy, as the techs got ready for the big demo day. They'd cordoned off spaces for lines to snake back and forth, in preparation for the huge influx of eager gamers. Aran couldn't help feeling smug about his personal invite. Sure, he knew Spark was just being gracious— he was too smart to read anything into it, which was maybe why she'd invited him in the first place—but it still felt good.

He spotted Spark's bright hair immediately, and veered over to where she was talking with one of the techs, a woman with a serious expression in her brown eyes.

"I agree, fifteen systems aren't enough," Spark was saying. "But it's all we get. I don't have that much pull with the company, as you know." She turned to Aran with a smile. "Hi! Glad you made it. Aran, this is Vonda, our lead on the floor today. Vonda, if you have a system ready to go, I've got you a tester."

Vonda nodded. "Over here."

"Thanks," Aran said.

He was torn between wanting to talk to Spark and diving into the FullD. Spark's smile deepened.

"Go ahead. You can tell me what you think after you play."

"I'll do that," Aran said.

He followed Vonda to where a gleaming FullD system sat, humming softly under the bright lights. She handed him a helmet and gloves.

"You know your way around an interface?" she asked.

"Yeah."

Aran slipped on the gloves and flexed his fingers. The fit was good, and the LEDs shone like tiny bits of rainbow. He slid into the chair and pulled the helmet on. Geared up and ready to go.

"Right then," Vonda said. "Give a yell if you get stuck."

He lifted one hand in acknowledgement, then turned his attention to the visor screen. The letter *F*, made of golden flame, took up most of his vision. With the flick of his index finger, Aran activated the game.

Moody, mysterious music played through the helmet. Words appeared, glowing and golden across the black background.

WELCOME TO FEYLAND

A VirtuMax Production

Version 1.1

A shiver of excitement ran down Aran's spine. There was nothing like the thrill of entering a new game for the first time. He hoped Feyland would live up to its hype and pull him into the supposedly brilliant simulation of a fantastical world —and that the holes and cheats wouldn't be too obvious. Half of the fun of running new content was the game, sure, but the other half was trying to get behind the interface, game the game as it were.

Words scrolled across the screen.

FEYLAND: A wondrous place where adventure awaits. Alone, or with other bold adventurers, seek out glory and riches, or pledge yourself in service to the greater good. This fabled land needs your skills and prowess to avert the dark shadows of the Neverwhere. Do you have the strength to prevail, or will you fail, as so many champions have before? Prove yourself in the epic game of Feyland!

The letters deepened to crimson, then scattered into ashy fragments, whirling away as the music rose. For a split second, a pair of eyes glowed from the shadows. Nice touch, giving the opening sequence just a hint of creepiness.

The screen changed, showing a character-creation interface. He skimmed over the possibilities. Even though he wanted to linger, to carefully read the descriptions of the various classes and their abilities, he didn't have the time. Right now, his job was to get in-game and start poking at the edges of the programming. The best way to do that was to choose a heavy-combat character in order to minimize time lost to dying.

He scrolled past the lightly armored magic users. He wouldn't be playing a Spellcaster or Healing Priest this time around. Partway through the medium combat classes, his eye was caught by a jaunty-looking avatar classified as a Saboteur. Aran paused, then shook his head and continued on to the heavily armored melee fighters. The limited choices of Knight, Mercenary, and Warrior seemed boring. He glanced back up at the rapier-wielding character dressed in dark blue and burgundy.

Saboteur, now… wasn't that his specialty?

Before he could second-guess his impulse, he lifted his finger and chose the character class. The Saboteur expanded to fill his vision.

SABOTEUR: A tricky character, the Saboteur's loyalties are not always easy to define. Skilled in use of the rapier and knives, this class has a range of stealth and misdirection skills.

Perfect.

Aran quickly modified the basic avatar, giving him a slender build—all the better for sneaking around—and skin a shade darker than his own. Too bad there wasn't an option to add an indigo streak to his character's hair.

At the naming prompt, he entered his standard onscreen name of Ebon.

Character complete. Enter game?

It only took a flick of his fingers to signal *yes*, and Aran paused a second to admire the smooth response of the gaming gloves. The real test would be in-game, but so far he had to admit the FullD system impressed him.

A brassy blare of trumpets filled his ears, and the visor screen flared with golden light. For a moment he felt as though he was falling through space, complete with a dizzy, disorienting clutch in his stomach.

He willed his senses to settle, and squeezed his eyes tight. When he opened them again, his character stood in the center of a clearing surrounded by white-barked trees, a summer-blue sky overhead. Velvety mosses cushioned his feet, and he was encircled by a ring of mushrooms, their scarlet caps dotted with white. A narrow path led from the clearing into the trees, their trunks graceful columns, their leaves shimmering silver in the faint breeze.

A breeze he could feel against his cheek. Wondering, Aran tilted his face up. Yes, he really felt the brush of air against his skin. It was almost as if he were standing there in person, instead of his digitally-created avatar. Even though he'd seen the demo last night—and Spark had been great—it hadn't prepared him for the actual *feel* of the game. VirtuMax had seriously outdone themselves.

Still, he had work to do. He was a Saboteur, after all. With a wry smile, Aran brought up the keyboard and typed in his most reliable hacker script. About half the games he cracked ran on an old-style operating system with more holes than a pierced-out goth.

No luck this time; the game scene remained unchanged, the graphics a solid wall between him and the programming. Good thing he had more than a few ways to pick apart the bytes.

The minutes ticked by, and each command he entered proved useless. Aran's chest tightened. This was his one chance to slide behind the programming before the game released, and he was skewing badly toward failure.

Okay, then. Maybe he'd get some insight into what else to try by playing forward. The path through the trees beckoned. Was it the only option?

Aran turned and picked a different part of the woods. He stepped out of the mushroom circle and strode forward—

Only to find himself back in the middle of the ring again. Another try in the opposite direction earned him the same result. VirtuMax had plugged any holes in the opening sequence code. If he had more time he'd try to unravel the edges, but not now.

Senses primed, he left the circle again, this time heading down the path. Fallen leaves softened his footsteps, and dappled light slanted between the trees. It was peaceful, and Aran didn't trust it one bit.

Still, no creatures leaped out at him with weapons bared, or charged through the underbrush, growling. The forest thinned and he stepped out from under the trees into a green meadow. The path curved, leading toward a storybook cottage; the kind of place where either a kindly woman or a wicked hag lived. Sometimes both, in the same person.

Aran called up his hacker scripts again. When he ran the third one, the air of Feyland rippled, and he glimpsed something behind the pastoral scene. Something glittering and dark.

What the hell was that?

Swallowing back a sudden jab of fear, he tried the code again. Nothing.

Nothing left to do but go farther into the game. Before heading to the cottage, he reviewed his character's combat skills, memorizing the few moves his Saboteur came equipped with. A couple stabs and slices, a dodge-and-disappear, and a distance knife throw. Hopefully they'd be adequate to deal with whatever creatures he might meet in battle.

A bird swooped overhead, singing. The meadow grasses, scattered with yellow and blue flowers like something out of a famous painting, riffled in the breeze. Still, he couldn't get that foreboding sense off his shoulders. Something was watching him—and waiting.

"Mr. Cole?" Vonda's voice sounded over his headset, roughened with static. "How's it going in there?"

"Good," Aran said. "It's an amazing place."

"You've got another twenty minutes to enjoy it before I need you to log off," she said.

"Right. I'll finish up. Just let me know when."

Time was funny in-game, but he was still surprised by how quickly it had gone. His stomach knotted. This was his chance, and so far he had nothing to show for it. *Way to go, mister supreme hacker.*

He didn't have time to waste standing around listening to his own self-doubt. Shutting up the mocking voice, Aran strode forward to the little cottage. Sunlight sparked off its diamond-paned windows and made the whitewashed walls and golden thatch shine brightly.

Something crouched on the front step; a creature that made Aran's steps slow. As he got closer he saw it was a hunched goblin with sharp teeth, wearing a blood-red cap and stained leather jerkin. The faint scent of rotting flowers wafted to Aran's nose.

The goblin stood, his clawed fingers clasped about a long-handled axe, his malicious gaze fixed on Aran. Taking a deep breath, Aran drew his knives.

Instead of attacking him, the goblin spoke, his voice rough as old hinges.

"Greetings, mortal," the creature said.

Aran rolled his weight onto the balls of his feet and considered how to answer. Maybe the goblin was a quest-giver of some kind, though there weren't many clues. Feyland was surprisingly scarce with the information given out to players. He supposed it was part of the immersive appeal, but most games provided at least a sense of the basics, if not full-on tutorials. This kind of confusing approach wasn't going to fly with a lot of casual gamers. What had VirtuMax been thinking?

The goblin tapped his ugly fingers, but gave no sign that he was planning to get violent.

"Hello," Aran said at last, bracing himself.

"Ah! It speaks." The goblin sneered at him. "What do you seek, Eron the Adventurer?"

A chill gripped the back of Aran's neck. "What did you call me?"

That was freaky. Sure, maybe he'd misspelled his usual avatar name, keying in Eron instead of Ebon. It still sounded uncomfortably close to his real name. Was Spark playing a practical joke on him?

"You seek to explore beyond the framework of Feyland," the goblin said, ignoring his question. "We can aid you."

Aran blinked. The conversation had just gone completely surreal. He was *not* having a chat with a character in-game about how to hack the game. No way.

"Aren't you supposed to give me a quest or something?" he asked.

"I offer you a way into the Realm. Into the world that lies beyond this one." The goblin waved his clawed hand at the cottage and peaceful meadow. "Do you accept?"

The wind stilled, the singing of birds muted. Aran's heartbeat sounded loud in his ears. For some reason, the question felt way more important than a simple step in a game.

"I do," he said. The words rang out like the clang of bells, hanging in the air, and he flinched.

"Good." The goblin bared his sharp teeth. "At the dark of the moon we will come and show you the way. Be ready, mortal. Midnight approaches."

Before Aran could say anything, the goblin disappeared. The wind went back to ruffling the grasses, and birds chirped merrily at the edge of the forest. Lungs tight, Aran made himself take a deep breath. That had been the weirdest gameplay he'd ever experienced.

And he still hadn't cracked a single line of Feyland's code.

Desperation edging his thoughts, he called up the keyboard interface and entered every possible hack he could think of. Nothing—not even that weird flicker he'd gotten earlier. It was as if the game was built on some kind of entirely new operating system, configured in ways he couldn't quite grasp.

"Ready to come out?" Vonda asked, her voice still broken by static.

Not at all, but what else could he do?

Fingers heavy, he gave the command to log out of Feyland. That same golden light flared, making his stomach twist. Then his ordinary senses returned. He was sitting in the FullD sim chair, the hubbub of the Expo Hall rising as the convention-goers flooded in.

He pulled off the helmet and stood. A wave of dizziness hit him, and he grabbed the back of the sim chair to steady himself. The fluorescent lights were too bright, and he squinted against the glare.

A long line of people waited to try the gaming systems. Spark stood by the main VirtuMax table, holding a stack of glossy images: promo pics of herself, simming. Seeing that he was off the system, she set them down and came over.

"What did you think of Feyland?" she asked.

"It was… really different." He shook his head, trying to clear it.

Her dark blue eyes fixed intently on him. "How so?"

"The immersion was amazing. I felt like I was actually there, you know?"

"I know. What else?"

He dropped his gaze to the dull beige carpet, avoiding her scrutiny. No way was he going to confess he'd spent his time in-game attempting to hack behind the interface.

"Um. Unexpected creatures." Total understatement.

"Did you get to any questlines?"

"Hey." He glanced back up. "I need to check in at the volunteer center. And you have about a million autographs to sign."

She looked at the waiting autograph seekers, then back to him. "I'd like to talk with you more, though. Lunch?"

He blinked. Spark Jaxley was inviting him to lunch?

"Sure."

"Great." Her mouth quirked up into a smile. "Come up to the VirtuMax VIP suite. Number 504. I'll tell my guys to let you in."

"Yo, Spark! Time to get to work," Vonda called, waving toward the table.

Fans were stacked up ten deep already, the ones in front giving Aran bitterly envious looks. He could practically hear them wondering who this guy was, taking up their idol's attention and keeping her from the essential task of signing her name and making small talk with them.

"I have to go," Spark said. "See you later."

Wonderful. He'd be stepping into the heart of VirtuMax security, carrying secrets that could get him in serious trouble. Watching Spark swing her magenta hair back and sit down at the table, Aran found that he couldn't wait.

CHAPTER FIVE

S<small>WEET MUSIC PLAYED</small> through the shadowed meadows and shivered through the silver-leaved oaks of the Dark Realm. Perched upon her tangled throne, the Dark Queen smiled.

The nixie combing her hair beside a moonlit stream paused, then bared her rows of sharp, serrated teeth. The wisps in the brackish swamps danced and swirled, leaving blue streaks of luminescence in the air. Moths with sightless eyes on pale wings fluttered helplessly, trapped in sticky, black-stranded webs.

"Well done, Codcadden," the queen said to the redcap goblin hunched in a bow before her. "When the moon shutters her face to the mortal world, you will fetch this human who has freely agreed to enter the realm."

"My lady," the goblin said. "How shall we bring him hither?"

"Send me." The Huntsman lifted his horned head. "My hunt has brought many a mortal across that boundary, and my hounds grow restless."

"No," the queen said. "I do not want him to arrive fickle-minded and wits-wandering from riding with the Wild Hunt. Three goblins and the Enchanted Sack shall do. After all, the mortal is willing."

"As my lady wishes."

The Huntsman returned to his vigil, his red-eyed hounds curling about him. The goblin before the throne bowed even lower, until his nose brushed the silken mosses.

"Go," the queen said. "Be assured of my favor. Your clan is welcome at the feasting tonight."

The goblin departed, not daring to glance at his ruler's face. The queen's moods were fickle of late, and the wrong tilt of the head or set of the mouth could send her into a rage. *Perhaps*, he thought, *this new mortal could set things aright*.

In the shadows behind the throne, the court musicians played softly. The music quieted as a weary-faced man stilled his guitar and stepped up beside the queen.

"My lady," he said. "Are you indeed set upon this course?"

"Bard Thomas." The look she turned on him was full of frost and midnight. "Do you think to barter for yet another mortal's life? Your human ways grow tiresome, and I begin to regret our bargain."

"Forgive me. I shall not speak of it again."

He made her a deep bow, then backed away, returning the sweet notes of his guitar to the music weaving about the court. The feasting tables were laid, platters heaped with delicacies for the ethereal and hideous denizens of the Dark Court to dine upon. Tall candelabras lined the tables, their flames unearthly still despite the night breeze. Gossamer-winged faerie maids laughed and danced, while black-haired creatures growled and slavered from the shadows.

The Dark Queen surveyed her court, then let her awareness expand to the very edge of her realm. On one side she was bounded by brightness, on the other, the newly rebuilt boundary between the Realm of Faerie and the human world.

Rebuilt, yes, but not without chinks in that obdurate wall. Her passage through might be barred for the moment, but soon enough she would hold the mortal key.

Two hours later, Spark's hand cramped and ached from signing autographs. She'd known it would, but she still refused to use a stamp, or pre-printed photos. Sure, VirtuMax had made her their spokesmodel, but the fans were way more important to her than the company. It was important to keep the whole fame thing as real as possible—for everyone involved.

Rubbing her palm with her left thumb, she let her security guys do their job and escort her with minimal drama out of the Expo Hall. Once they reached the corridor outside, she realized how incredibly noisy it had been on the floor. Her ears still hummed from the aftermath.

She sighed, and Burt gave her a sympathetic glance.

"Two more days, Miss Jaxley."

She wished her security team would call her by her first name, but they were sticklers for following protocol. It was one of the reasons VirtuMax hired the company in the first place. After a couple of tries she'd quit trying to argue about it.

"One day, really," she said. "The con's over after the big lunch panel tomorrow."

After that, she was off to do a string of appearances at game emporiums and super-stores up and down the coast. The week of the official FullD release was packed with multiple events, plus a daytime news show interview and a guest spot at Bella Boingo's sold-out stadium concert. SimCon was a vacation in comparison.

"Your guest has arrived, miss," Joe, the guard at the door of her VIP suite, said. "He's waiting inside."

"Thanks."

Right. She'd almost forgotten that she'd invited Aran to have lunch with her. It had been an impulse, but something about his reaction to playing Feyland had been off. And Feyland plus weirdness wasn't something she could overlook.

Aran was reclining in a big white beanbag in the main room, texting on his messenger. When he saw her, he tucked the device away and jumped to his feet. His smile really was cute, and she liked how the corners of his eyes crinkled from it.

"Hey," she said. "Sorry to make you wait."

"No stress. They give you way more comfortable chairs than us peons in the volunteer room. It's good to slack after running around all morning."

"You're a volunteer?"

For some reason she'd thought he was on the con staff. Maybe because of his self-assurance, or his calm manner. It was refreshing to spend time with someone her own age who didn't freak out in her presence. The rest of the Feyguard excepted.

"Yeah," he said, "I'm a gofer."

"So you're a local? Come eat, and tell me what I should see on my half-day off."

Though part of her had considered spending her partial day off asleep, she also hated to miss seeing new places. This city, despite the dreary weather, seemed interesting.

She led him to the small table where the catered lunch was set up. Nothing special—turkey wraps with veggies, chips, and her favorite chocolate bars, imported from Belgium.

Aran snagged a soda from the assortment on the table, then took his own chair. He popped the top, the crisp sound loud in the quiet of the suite.

"Do you have an umbrella?" he asked. "A raincoat?"

"Probably."

"You don't know?" He shot her a look. "Or did you leave it at home?"

"It's complicated."

She took a bite of her lunch, suddenly embarrassed. Now that she was paying attention, she could tell Aran's clothes were a little too worn to be fashionable. She'd bet credits that he'd worn the same jeans yesterday. Which was a normal thing, except that she knew what it was like to have one decent pair, and no money for more. And she knew that slight air of defiance that came from wearing the only presentable clothing you had.

"I travel a lot," she said. "All over the world. When it's winter here, it's summer someplace else."

"That must be prime, seeing all those countries." His voice held a note of yearning.

She didn't ask him if he'd traveled much. She didn't need to. It was clear Aran wanted to go places, but hadn't. Yet.

"Thing is," she continued, "sometimes I don't even know where VirtuMax is sending me until I get there. I have an assistant that knows my schedule weeks in advance. She packs everything I need and makes sure it's waiting for me on arrival."

His eyes widened. "Don't you have anything that goes with you? Favorite shirt or something?"

"I have a few possessions, but I prefer to travel light. Makes things easier."

She couldn't afford to get too attached, to things *or* people. Two and a half years on the road had taught her that. Whether it was a broken heart when she had to leave her first boyfriend behind, or the treasured necklace that had been stolen from her bags, she'd had to learn how to let go.

"Since you were coming here, I'm sure you have a rain-coat," he said. "Dig it out, because the best parts of this city are outside."

As they finished eating lunch, Aran described the high-lights of his home town: the outdoor fair, the famous skyscraper, the hidden cove by the sea, reachable only by walking along old train tracks.

"And of course," he said, "no visit is complete without sampling the ice cream stands all over the place."

"Isn't it a little cold for that?" She pushed her empty plate away and started unwrapping one of the chocolate bars, the purple foil smooth under her fingers.

"We don't care." He grinned at her. "That's why they're combo vendors. Ice cream and coffee. Or hot chocolate, if you prefer."

"I do." She broke a square off the bar and offered it to him. "How could you tell?"

"Lucky guess."

He accepted the chocolate, then reached over and took her hand. It was a natural gesture, and she was too surprised to pull away.

"You've been rubbing your palm this whole time," he said. "Let me."

"I have?" She knew her hand ached, but hadn't paid much attention.

It was bold of him to reach out like that, yet it made her feel normal—like she wasn't the untouchable sim star every-body else saw. She'd stop him if he pushed her boundaries too far, but the novelty of his gesture kept her silent, and strangely content.

His fingers wrapped around the back of her hand, strong and warm, while his thumb massaged her open palm. It was a delicious feeling, in all kinds of ways. Blood rushed through her, while the ache in her hand eased. She let out a long breath, and he stopped.

"Too hard?"

"No—it's perfect." She probably should ask him to stop, but it felt so good.

Not just the massage, which was great, but the sensation of touch, of someone's skin against her own. She felt like a drooping plant getting much-needed water.

Finally, he stopped and pulled his hand away. It was hard to tell with his dusky skin, but she thought he was blushing.

"Better?" he asked.

"Much. Maybe I should hire you to come on tour as my hand massager. Put you on the VirtuMax payroll." She was only half joking.

Something flashed through his eyes, and he sat back a little. She didn't know what she'd said, but the closeness she'd felt between them was gone.

"I need to get back to work," he said, tugging on the badge slung around his neck. "Thanks for lunch."

Disappointment curled through her, along with the realization she hadn't had a chance to ask him more about his time in Feyland.

"Can't you stay a bit longer?"

He stood. "Sorry—my shift is about to start and I don't want to be late."

Clearly she didn't have time now to ask probing questions about his in-game experience, but she wasn't going to let this go. As a member of the Feyguard, she couldn't.

"Are you free tonight?" she asked.

"Maybe." His tone was cautious.

"VirtuMax is throwing a party," she said, trying to sound casual. "If you want, I'll put you on the guest list. Bring a friend."

Did he have a girlfriend? She didn't like how the thought stabbed. Well, she'd find out—and it wasn't like she could start dating the guy herself. She was leaving first thing Monday morning.

"That would be great," he said, and sounded like he meant it.

She walked him over to the door. They stood there awkwardly for a moment, not quite touching.

"See you later, then," she said. "It's in suite 204."

"Okay. Later."

He met her gaze, and something in his dark eyes made a little flame flicker to life in the middle of her chest. Then he was gone, closing the door softly behind him.

Dammit. She was *not* falling for some cute gamer guy she knew nothing about. Even if he seemed nice and had rubbed her hand.

Spark leaned her forehead against the closed door, feeling the vibrations of the con rumbling through the building. She didn't want to turn around and go back into the empty suite, breathe in the stale air of loneliness, and eat the rest of the chocolate by herself.

But she did.

Aran's feet were sore from working the Expo Hall the rest of the afternoon. At five o'clock, he and two other volunteers walked through the big room, announcing they were closing up for the night. All the convention-goers needed to leave before the main doors locked at five thirty. The vendors would have one door available to them, but that would close at six.

"Doors reopen at ten," Aran called. "Everybody out."

Two gray-haired guys were arguing at a table filled with

old-school RPG books and board games. One of them picked up a figurine and brandished it.

"The introduction of the Elbeck was the worst idea, ever! From then on, the game totally dived."

"Lies. Without the Elbeck, the entire storyline makes no sense. Dude, you're an idiot."

Aran leaned forward, ready to intervene if things got violent. The one guy raised his hand, and Aran started to sprint over, only to relax as the Elbeck-hater clapped the other fellow on the back.

"Come on," he said, tossing the figurine down on the table. "Let's go get a beer."

"Right on."

The two men headed for the exit, still arguing companionably. Behind them, a couple sporting tufted ears and long, striped tails darted, playing a growling game of tag on their way out.

Gamers. Aran shook his head, but couldn't help smiling. These crazy people were his tribe—even though he'd gone over to what some of them would call the dark side. He felt too stuffy, dressed in his jeans and SimCon shirt. Tonight, the blue streak was going back in his hair.

He met Bix at the info table up front, the Expo Hall strangely quiet as the vendors closed up.

"I'm so ready for fun," Bix said. "Think we can get into some more parties? Maybe we'll meet up with Cyndee and Pema again."

Aran had to think for a second, "Right—warrior princess and robo-enforcer-girl."

"You have to admit, they were pretty flawless."

There was only one girl on Aran's mind, and nobody else at the convention could even come close.

"If you want to go to a party," he said, "how about VirtuMax's?"

Bix snorted. "Right. You have to be on the list for that one. No sliding in just because of our shirts and badges."

"I got us on the list."

"What?" Bix stared at him, his eyes comically wide. "Not true."

"Yes true."

"Woot!" Bix started dancing around, waving his long arms. "I can't believe it—this is so prime!"

Aran couldn't help smiling at his friend's excitement. He shared it, though he drew the line at dancing like a maniac.

It would be good to see Spark one more time before the con ended. And she had mentioned her half-day off. If he invited her to see the city with him, would she come? His pulse sped at the thought.

Bix finally stopped dancing. "When does the party start?"

"I'm not sure. Not too early."

"What should we wear? Like, costumes, or just normal clothes? Do you think Spark Jaxley will be there?"

"No doubt. Come on." Aran headed for the exit.

Somehow, the moment to reveal his budding friendship with Spark had come and then gone. Now it felt too late.

"I think I'll be NinjaQuad," Bix said. "I can use my brother's costume."

"Will it fit?" Outside the Expo Hall they took a right, back toward Gofer Central.

"I'll make it fit. What are you wearing?"

"Let's grab our stuff and go home," Aran said. "We can figure out it out, eat something, and get back here within a couple hours. The party won't get going until then, anyway."

He didn't feel like arguing with Bix about wearing a costume. It would be enough to re-dye his hair and wear his Tinz shirt—his favorite band. He'd actually bought the shirt, though he'd climbed the fence with a couple of friends to sneak into the concert. Good times.

So, no costume. For one thing, he didn't have one, and for another, he wanted Spark to recognize him. He had a feeling she'd be herself, too—though the room would probably be full of magenta-haired gamer girls.

Which meant going as Spark Jaxley was the perfect disguise.

CHAPTER SIX

LOUD MUSIC THROBBED through suite 204, along with flashing lights from the temporary dance floor. Spark sipped a glowing cup of VirtuMax-red punch, watched the multicolored lights play over the partygoers, and tried not to stare at the door. Just because Aran said he'd come didn't mean he would. Or that it meant anything if he did. Being put on the guest list wasn't the same thing as actually going on a date.

Get it together, she told herself, heading to the refreshment table. It was ridiculous to waste time dreaming over a guy. Even if he was cute, and good company.

She grabbed a plate and put a couple of cookies on it to give herself something to do, then went to lean against the wall again. Luckily, in the semi-dim light, it was hard for people to see that she was the actual Spark Jaxley. So far she'd counted eight other people dressed like her—and not all of them were women.

Vonda joined her, costumed as one of her favorite anime creatures, complete with six purple arms. Three of them held glasses of punch, and Spark hoped the mechanics stayed solid. She didn't want red glow spilled on her.

"Demos went well today," Vonda said. "We managed to get more than two-thirds of the line through."

"That's a record. I think all of them came and got autographs."

"How's the hand?"

"Good enough." Spark shrugged, glad the low light hid her expression. Aran's mini-massage had helped. "What did you think of the guy I invited to come early?"

Vonda tilted her head. "Cute. But you knew that already."

"I meant his gaming."

Spark took a sip of punch, even though she hated how the glow clung to people's lips for a moment afterward. If she had infrared vision, she'd probably be able to see people's whole digestive tracts lit up. Disturbing thought.

"He obviously knew his way around a sim-system. Beyond that, I couldn't say. I was too busy getting everything else set up. Where'd you meet him?"

"Here, at the con. He's a volunteer. When he logged out, did you notice anything... off?"

"Hm." Vonda crossed two of her arms. "Maybe, yeah. I didn't tag it right away, but after watching hundreds of people come out of Feyland today, his reaction was a little strange. No smiles, no gushing praise. Or even the opposite. He was real quiet when he walked away."

The confirmation gave Spark a twinge. She'd been right— and she doubly hoped Aran would come to the party tonight. Pointed questions were in order, and she wouldn't let him distract her this time.

"Is there a problem?" Vonda asked.

"No. Just wondering."

"You could ask him about his gaming experience yourself. He's over there by the couches."

"What?" Spark's heart gave a thump, then settled back into a faster rhythm. She scanned the clots of people standing at the far end of the room. "Are you sure?"

"Since he's not in costume, yes. There," she pointed with yet another arm, "next to the warrior babe."

"I see him."

And she wished she hadn't. The girl he stood by was giving him a possessive look, and she was gorgeous—all lush curves and pouty lips, the way Spark would never be. As she watched, the warrior babe curled her arm around Aran's.

He wasn't wearing his glasses, which was why she hadn't spotted him immediately. Without the dark frames his sharp cheekbones stood out.

"Go talk to him," Vonda said.

"I don't—"

"Come *on*. You're Spark Jaxley. Here, I'll take those." Vonda grabbed her plate and cup of punch, which Spark was happy to give up without a fight.

She tucked her hair behind one ear. Sure, she was a star, but that didn't mean she was flawlessly self-confident every waking moment.

"I'm waiting." Vonda started tapping her foot in a theatrical manner.

"You think being my part-time manager means you can boss me around?"

"Yep."

"Fine."

Spark lifted her chin and made her way past a group of gyrating dancers, toward the couches. She almost veered away when Aran's girlfriend whispered something in his ear. Then he saw her and smiled. A real smile, not a star-struck one. So she kept going until she was standing in front of him.

"Hi," she said. "Glad you came." Even if he'd brought his date.

"Wouldn't miss it." He glanced at his girlfriend. "Pema, I'd like you to meet—"

"Spark Jaxley," Pema said. "Decent costume, if a bit uninspired."

As if the warrior princess showing lots of skin was an original idea.

"Hey." Aran untangled his arm from Pema's grasp. "This is actually the real—"

"Aran, man, you have *got* to come over here," a tall, gangly guy in a too-small costume interrupted, grabbing Aran's shoulder from behind. "Cyndee just met one of the VirtuMax techs!"

"Hold on, Bix," Aran said as his friend started moving away. "I want you to meet—"

"Well, come soon. I gotta get back, before Cyndee decides he's a better date."

"He's a *cute* VirtuMax tech?" Pema asked. "I'm with ya. Later, Aran."

With a swish of her hips, Pema turned and followed the tall guy away, leaving Spark blinking at Aran.

"Wait," she said. "Pema's not your girlfriend?"

She felt as if someone put the room on pause as she waited for his answer.

"No. I just met her yesterday."

The lights flashed, red and green and purple, and the music pulsed through the air, kick-starting Spark's smile.

"You met a lot of people yesterday," she said, trying not to grin too much.

"But only one that I'd like to know better," he said. "Want to dance?"

"Sure."

They found a corner of the floor, and she was glad to see that Aran was a good dancer. Nothing too flashy, nothing too geeky, although she had to laugh a little when they started copying one another's robo-dance moves.

The DJ put on a slow song, and Spark hesitated. Then Aran opened his arms, and she went into them. She slipped her arms around his shoulders, and their bodies gently bumped as they swayed together. It was straight out of a too-sweet movie, but she didn't care.

She was just a girl, dancing with a boy, and everything in the world was right.

The music stopped too soon. She leaned her head against his chest a moment longer, counting his breaths.

She pulled back a little and touched the dash of indigo in his black hair. "Is this new? I like it."

"I just redid it. My rebel streak."

"I think it goes deeper than your hair."

She could picture him, riding midnight streets on a sleek grav-cycle, pushing the speed limit, flying over the horizon toward dawn and freedom.

"Maybe." His expression was shuttered.

"Break time," the DJ announced. "Grab some refreshments, and meet me back here in ten!"

Spark stepped out of Aran's arms as the room lights came up.

"Want to get some punch?" she asked.

"Not really. That glow weirds me. Maybe just a glass of water."

"Let's go to the kitchen." She tilted her head to the half-hidden door in the corner of the suite. "That's where they keep the high-class beverages. You know, water, fruit juice."

"Caffeinated drinks?"

"Definitely."

Spark led him around the plastic ferns in the corner, and they slipped into the empty kitchen. The remains of frantic party-readying were evident in the empty food containers scattered over the counters and the glowing red puddle of punch in the sink.

"I think there's a coffee maker in here somewhere," Spark said.

"I'm good with soda."

She opened the fridge, and Aran snagged a silver can of high-octane soda.

"You planning on staying up all night?" she asked.

"Maybe. If the company keeps being this good."

"Does that line actually work for you?" She had to admit, though, it had. A little.

He laughed. "Hey, if it's true, it's not a line."

She rolled her eyes. But no matter how much she liked

him, she had some questions she needed to ask before he distracted her again.

"I want to hear more about your experience in Feyland," she said, trying to keep her tone light. "We didn't get enough of a chance to talk about what you thought of the game-play."

"I told you—it was interesting."

"That's not very detailed." A shiver of unease went through her. "What, exactly, did you do in there?"

He set his soda on the counter, then took her hands. "That's not important. Have you ever seen the sun rise over the sea?"

"You're avoiding my question."

"Look. I'm trying to ask you out. We'll have plenty of time to talk as I show you the city. That is, if your keepers will let you go."

She couldn't help the pleased glow that warmed her from within.

"If they don't, I'll fire them."

"Good."

He held her gaze and leaned forward. The promise of a kiss tingled in the space between them—and the kitchen door swung open, letting in a blare of music. And Burt.

"Everything all right in here, Miss Jaxley?"

It had been, until he walked in.

"Sure," she said. "Burt, you remember Aran, from lunch?"

"Of course." His voice was flat.

"Hey," Aran said.

His eyes were guarded. For a long moment he and Burt just looked at each other. If they had hackles, she was sure they'd be raised.

"Burt," she said, "Aran's going to take me out to see the city. I'll be back after sunrise."

"I don't think so." Burt crossed his arms.

"I'll take good care of her," Aran said.

"That's what I'm worried about."

"Stop it." She stepped between them. "I can take care of myself, thank you very much. Burt, you're my security team leader, not my dad. Besides, I know the protocol."

Aran raised his brows. "Protocol?"

"I'm only allowed to be gone four hours, have to activate the locater in my wrist-chip to a specific frequency, and check in every half-hour." In some ways, having a security team was worse than parents.

"Being a super-celebrity seems pretty tweaked, you know that?"

"Oh, I know."

All too well. But tonight she wanted to shut away that part of her life and be an ordinary girl.

"Hold out your hand," Burt said, gesturing to Aran. "Let me see that chip."

"So you can short it out?" Aran asked. "No thanks."

"Mr. Cole, if you don't want me to throw you out this very moment, it's a requirement."

Aran hesitated. She could see his throat move as he swallowed. Then he rolled up his sleeve and extended his arm, wrist up.

Burt leaned forward, gave a grunt, and with his thumbnail flicked the chip completely off Aran's wrist. It sparkled, turning in the air, before Burt caught it in his meaty fist.

"Burt! His chip—you can't do that." Turning to Aran, she

grabbed his hand, inspecting his skin for blood. "Are you all right?"

"Sorry, Spark," he said. "It was a fake."

"What?" A spurt of anger heated her blood, and she dropped his wrist. "Are you a fake, too? Is your name even Aran, or is this some game you're playing?"

"No." He gave her a pained look. "This is real."

"Aran Myeong Cole," Burt said. "American father, Korean mother. Ostensibly lives at 1418 Circle Court, with two siblings and both parents. Graduated from high school two years early, and was accepted on full scholarship to several elite colleges. Attended none of them, due to—"

"All right," Aran said, his voice raised and uneven. "Real enough for you? I think I'm done here."

He turned and started for the door.

"Wait." Spark caught his arm. "You can't just leave."

"It was nice meeting you," he said. "I'll always be a fan."

"No." Her fingers tightened. "We are not finished. I need to know what you did today, in Feyland."

Aran jerked his head up, his pupils wide. "I told you. I explored the world a little bit. That's it."

"He's lying," Burt said.

"Aran, listen to me." She had no idea how to say this, especially in front of Burt. "The game is… different. Be careful."

Aran's brows drew together, and she could see the pulse beating fast in his neck. He glanced at Burt, then back to her.

"Goodbye, Spark."

Before she could react, he leaned in and brushed a kiss over her lips. Then he pulled away, out of her grasp, out the kitchen door, out of her life.

"Miss Jaxley—"

"Why did you do that?" She whirled on Burt. "The one guy who treated me like a real person, and you drove him away!"

"I'm sorry," he said. "It's my job. That boy has a criminal record for running drugs. And he was lying to you. You spending time with him was a no-go."

Great. She'd been all too right about Aran's rebel streak.

"I'm going back to my rooms."

She stalked past Burt, taking the other exit from the kitchen. If she had to walk back through the VirtuMax party, she would scream at the emptiness of it all.

Burt followed her without a word, just doing his job. Whether she wanted him to or not.

There was no escaping from her life. Not even by playing games, the way she used to do. Now her life was a huge, complex game, played on VirtuMax's system.

Well, that wasn't completely true. The world was bigger than the FullD, or the continent, or even the planet. There were worlds beyond worlds, and she had even seen one of them.

But even memories of haunting fey magic couldn't ease the aching of her human heart.

CHAPTER SEVEN

Aran slumped on the lumpy sofa in the Chowney's garage, his battered tablet in one hand. He'd turned the single wall-mounted heater on, but it did little to push back the chill. Even with a cup of ramen in his belly and his bulky black hoodie on, he couldn't get warm.

Everything in his life was sour. He'd gotten nowhere with hacking Feyland, he'd severely tweaked it with Spark—not that they'd had a chance of something real, anyway—and he'd just found out some guy on *buysimcheats.com* had undercut all his prices. He was down to twelve bucks, half of it in grimy change.

And he didn't even have his fake chip any more. It was a little thing, but it stung the back of his throat. He was out of choices, with nowhere left to go.

At the dark of the moon, we will come and take you... The goblin's words echoed through his mind. Aran scrolled through the calendars on his tablet until he found one that showed the phases of the moon. The dark of the moon was tomorrow.

His stomach tightened, although he knew nothing was going to happen. Feyland was just a game.

From outside the thin window he heard giggling. He immediately powered off his tablet, the blue glow fading until the garage was dark. Rising, he twitched open the thick, dusty curtain and could barely make out the figure of Bix trying to boost the robo-enforcer girl into his bedroom window.

"Just push it up," Bix whispered in a too-loud voice.

"I'm trying."

She shoved at the window, lost her balance, and the two of them toppled into the shrubbery. Aran winced at the crackle of breaking branches. No lights went on in the house, though Bix and Cyndee were smart enough to lie there quietly for a moment.

Still, they were going to be discovered, and Bix would regret it. His parents were strict. If they could, they'd confine him to his room until he left for college next fall.

Quiet as a shadow, Aran slipped out the door and into the yard.

"You two," he whispered.

"What?" Bix turned on the thin beam of a flashlight and shone it around. "Aran?"

"Come to the garage," Aran said.

Bix untangled himself from the shrubs and helped Cyndee out. When the three of them reached the musty darkness of the garage, Aran flicked his tablet back on, letting the blue light illuminate the room.

"Really?" He turned to Bix. "What do you think your parents will say when they discover you?"

Cyndee set a hand on her hip and scowled at Bix. "You said it was all flash for me to come over. I don't want no raging 'rents."

"You guys can stay here." Aran tilted his head toward the couch he slept on most nights.

"What about you?" Bix asked.

"I'm not sleepy," Aran lied. "Besides, I've got a date."

Right. An imaginary magenta-haired girl with a great laugh waited for him beside the sea. If only things were different. If only *he* were different, not forever marked by one naïve mistake that had cost him everything.

"Have fun," he said, scooping up his bag and tucking his tablet inside. "See you later, Bix."

"Thanks, man. Catch you at the con tomorrow?"

"Maybe."

Aran lifted his hand in farewell and went out into the empty night—made all the more bitter by the sound of Cyndee's laughter and Bix's answering murmur as he shut the door.

Aran spent some of his change at a late-night coffeehouse, idly flicking through the gaming headlines on his tablet. Once the place closed down he caught the last bus to the outskirts. It was just him and a guy who reeked of urine. Aran was glad to get off where the train tracks crossed the road.

He walked the rails, shining silvery gray in the first light of approaching dawn. Ahead, he could hear the waves swooshing back and forth over the gravelly beach.

The faint drizzle faded, leaving a sheen of water over the earth. He balanced on the glistening metal tracks, then took the cutoff through the bracken, his jeans wicking water from the evergreen leaves. Ahead of him, the hushing of the sea grew louder as the path dropped to the shore.

Aran followed the trail around the last hump of land, and the sea opened before him, all gray and moving like a vast, living creature. He drew in a deep breath, scented with salt and crushed ferns, and scrambled down to the stone-covered slice of shore.

Despite the dreariness of his life, his spirits rose. It was hard to be completely depressed at the secret cove, especially as the clouds turned silver, then pinkish gold. He walked along the water line, looking for treasure. Once he'd found an old glass fishing float, but most of the time only trash washed ashore.

Dingy Styrofoam and frayed bits of bright orange netting, bottle caps, and shredded plastic. Humans could be such careless, dirty things. Sometimes he'd bring a garbage bag and fill it, though he'd forgotten this time.

The debris wasn't enough to erase the wonder of the sunrise. He wandered over to a bleached driftwood log and perched there, not worrying about the damp. His jeans were wet anyway. Arms folded, he watched the sky brighten to white, then blue, until he had to turn his face away from the horizon and the burning golden ball of the sun.

Something caught his eye, right at the edge of the water, a flash of magenta almost as bright as Spark's hair. Timing his steps to the tide, Aran grabbed it—a stone, water-slick and gleaming, striated with bands of pink and darker purple. It wasn't the first agate he'd found on the beach, but it was the prettiest.

He cupped it in his palm, watching the colors fade as it dried, then slipped the stone into his pocket.

Without meaning to, he'd decided to return to SimCon for the last half-day. Bix expected him, and, hell, why not? He swallowed Spark's name, and turned his back to the rising sun.

"All is in readiness, my queen." The redcap goblin knelt before the tangled throne, eyes averted from his ruler's icy gaze. "Tonight we enter the mortal world and fetch the human."

The Dark Queen lifted her face to the star-dappled sky and inhaled deeply. Power tingled, almost within her grasp. The night tasted of wildness and lost dreaming.

Soon.

Spark opened her eyes, groggy and disoriented. For a second she had no idea where she was, and the anonymity of the hotel room didn't help. She'd woken in hundreds of rooms that looked just like this one: beige walls holding paintings of innocuous landscapes, soap-scented sheets, curtains that always let in a thick slab of light at the sides.

Then memory tumbled back into her brain. SimCon, and the rainy city she'd decided not to explore after all. And Aran.

She squeezed her eyes shut, letting brief regret wash over her, then stuck the feeling in a little box and locked it up tight.

Enough with the self-pity and tragic heroine bit. So she met a guy and it didn't work out. Welcome to life.

She wasn't much of a coffee drinker, but she called room service and ordered a mocha, along with their fruit-and-pastry plate. The food was waiting outside her door when she got out of the shower. One of Burt's guys was, too. Well, not directly outside, but sitting in the room across the hall with the door propped open. She didn't feel shy about not being dressed yet; after all, she was wrapped up in her thick bathrobe. If she let the security team bother her that much, she'd be a walking mess.

"Morning, Miss Jaxley," he said. "After the official luncheon, we'll be rolling out. If that's good with you?"

"Hi, Joe. And yeah, it's fine." No reason to stay around.

She grabbed her breakfast tray and locked the door behind her. While she ate, she scanned the entertainment headlines on her tablet. There—the report on SimCon. She skimmed over the pictures of herself, and read the article on Feyland with interest. The reporter had gotten a chance to try the FullD, and was full of praise for the immersive interface and creative quest lines.

Not that her job depended on whether the FullD was a success, since she was under contract to VirtuMax for the next two years. But she had that other job—the fey border patrol.

Spark switched to her messager. Though it was early, she hoped Jennet would be awake.

:*You up?*: she sent.

After a bite of scone and a sip of her mocha, Spark's messager pinged.

:Am now. Did you see that guy again?:

:His name's Aran. And no. That's done.:

:Sorry to hear it.: Jennet sent a sad face graphic, which, ironically, made Spark smile a little.

:So, what are the details about us being Feyguard?: Spark asked.

:Tam and I have been talking about it. We figure our job is to watch the interface between the game and the realm, since we're familiar with both. The Elder Fey didn't seal the realm off completely, so a few people are bound to slip through the cracks.:

:And our job is to get them before they stumble too far into the Realm of Faerie. But how will we know when we're needed?:

Like when someone who'd gone in-game behaved suspiciously. Was she just supposed to follow her intuition? But then what?

:I'm sure the Elder Fey have that covered. Somehow.:

:Reassuring. Creatures from another dimension got it handled, check.:

:Haha: Jennet wrote. *:Seriously, though, I'll keep talking it over with Tam. Game releases next week.:*

:As if I don't know it. My schedule's insane. Speaking of which, gotta go.:

:Later.:

Spark finished her breakfast, then checked the time. Vonda would be waiting for her on the floor in half an hour, and then there was the VirtuMax luncheon panel. Spark was one of the panelists, along with Mr. Chon—who'd taken over as lead developer for Feyland after Thomas died—and the graphics designer, and a few other people who'd dedicated years of their lives to the game.

She was just the candy in the window, although she'd been on the beta-test team. The trick was to deflect the questions about her fame and her life, twist them into questions about the game, and hand them over to the other panelists. She'd gotten pretty good at it. Though Feyland and the FullD were the company's biggest offering, Spark had helped debut plenty of other systems and sim games.

Instead of putting on her "Spark suit," the vaguely super hero-looking costume VirtuMax liked her to wear, she pulled on jeans and a black shirt. It was helpful for the panel, not to look too different. No matter what the PR people said.

A touch of makeup, not the heavy stage face she put on for the demo, and she was ready.

Her messager pinged again, this time with a note from Vonda.

:Yo, Spark. Ten minutes.:

:Coming,: Spark wrote back.

When she stepped into the hall, Joe was waiting to escort her down to the convention. Making her way through the hubbub of the Expo Hall, she tried not to look too closely at every lean and muscled guy with black hair. Even if Aran showed up, there was no point.

Ten feet into the room, she was mobbed with fans. Grateful for the distraction, Spark turned her attention to signing more autographs, answering questions, and letting Joe take the gifts thrust at her.

The morning sped by. Before she could catch her breath, Joe and Vonda did their crowd-management thing and got her into the room behind the banquet room, where the panel was gathering for lunch.

They wouldn't be eating in the main room during the panel, obviously. Nothing elegant about answering questions through a mouthful of food.

"Hello, Spark," Mr. Chon said, giving her a formal nod as she walked in. "How has the convention been?"

"Great." She smiled through the lie.

She was sorry Jennet's dad wasn't there instead. He and Mr. Chon didn't get along, especially after Mr. Carter stood up for the whole beta team and undermined Mr. Chon's authority. They both still worked for VirtuMax, but Jennet's dad was now lead on a new project, while Mr. Chon got Feyland.

"I hear the demo went well," he said.

Nice of him not to be there. She swallowed the words. "Yeah. Fun times. Hey, I'm going to grab a cup of tea. Good to see you."

She could play politician with the best of them, but she hoped Mr. Chon wouldn't be seated next to her on the panel. There were limits.

"Spark!" One of the younger VirtuMax employees, a guy named Wilo, waved from a nearby table. "Come join us."

"Will do. Let me grab my lunch."

She went to the buffet table and selected a box that supposedly contained a panini and a Caesar salad, then chose a beverage. Strong black tea, with milk and sugar—the way her Irish grandma used to drink. The taste was as comforting as going over to Nana's and sitting in her soft lap, getting her hair braided while Nana crooned old melodies into her ear. Too bad the feeling didn't last.

Wilo, a lead artist for VirtuMax, and Tia, a tech goddess,

were good company and didn't make Spark feel like she was some sort of distant diva. Their lively conversation helped lift her spirits. Too soon, lunch ended and the panel moderator began rounding everyone up.

"Spark," Vonda called, beckoning to her from the corner. "I need to talk to you."

Her voice held a suppressed urgency that made Spark frown as she walked over.

"What's going on?"

"I just found out VirtuMax flew in more guests for the panel. They decided the launch was too big for you to do solo and pulled a couple more gamers in."

"No." Spark's lunch turned to stone in her stomach. "Oh no. By a couple, you mean two, right? Please tell me it's not the Terribles."

Though it couldn't be anyone else. The Terabin twins were VirtuMax's second-place celebrities. They used to be the first, until VirtuMax hired Spark. A year older than she was, Roc and Cora hadn't taken well to losing their top billing. Or their cash bonuses from extra sponsorships. Any time she had to cross paths with them, things got nasty.

VirtuMax finally figured that out after the twins set up a "prank" that almost ended in severe injury for Spark. Though nothing could be proven, the company made sure to keep them far apart. Until now.

"It is." Vonda's gaze went past Spark, and her lips pinched together.

"Well, well." The voice behind her was like an ice cube sliding over Spark's skin. "It's the pink-haired punk. How special."

CHAPTER EIGHT

SPARK SLOWLY TURNED to see Roc and Cora Terabin standing shoulder to shoulder behind her. They were dressed identically, as usual, in one of their many gamer outfits. The current one was silver and violet, with sleek pants tucked into big black boots.

Even though they were fraternal twins, they liked to play up their physical similarities with a twist of gender ambiguity. Roc was taller, his face squarer, his voice deeper. Some people said he was handsome, with his chocolate-brown hair and amber eyes, but the flatness in his expression invalidated his superficial good looks.

His sister, Cora, wore platform boots—subtle, but enough to bring her closer to her brother's height. The eyeliner they both wore looked more flattering on him, though Spark wasn't about to say so. The less she spoke to the Terabins, the better.

She'd tried before to field their barbed words with snappy

comebacks. At the moment, though, the two of them felt like more than she could face.

"Ready?" the panel moderator called. "Showtime!"

The noise from the banquet room increased as the moderator opened the connecting door: conversations layered on monologues layered on laughter, the clink of silverware on plates, and clatter of ice in glasses.

Mr. Chon led the way, gesturing for Spark to follow. Vonda gave her arm a squeeze, but there was nothing she, or anyone, could do.

Pasting a smile on, Spark felt the crowd's attention veer toward them as the panel walked up to the stage and took their places at the long table. Microphones lined the white tablecloth, one in front of each name card, along with a bottle of water.

Spark found her name and sat down. She was at the center of the table, and someone had thought it would be a cute idea to put the Terabins on either side. Great.

Teeth bared, Roc took the seat on her right. Cora passed him, setting her hand on Spark's shoulder as she went by. Her sharp nails bit through the thin cotton of Spark's T-shirt, and Spark regretted not putting on her costume. One more layer of armor between her and the twins would have been nice, even if it was rubberized and a garish teal blue.

The moderator introduced them, and Mr. Chon gave a rambling introduction about VirtuMax's development of the FullD system, and the inspiration behind Feyland. Little did he know.

Spark kept her elbows tucked in and her knees close together, careful not to stray into enemy territory. Her best defense was to act nonchalant, though her palms were sweating.

"I'll let our amazing gamers talk about how it feels inside the sim," Mr. Chon said. "Spark, why don't you start?"

She felt Cora's glare. The other girl had never forgiven her for being younger, faster, and better. Not to mention a more pleasant human being. The Terabins came from a wealthy family, and stories about their arrogance and demands were legendary, even before Spark joined VirtuMax. Afterwards, they had gotten worse.

"As a lot of you know from playing the demo yesterday," Spark said, "the FullD interface is the best sim immersion yet. I know we've been waiting a long time for a game that *feels* real, and that game is Feyland."

Her words earned a couple cheers and a patter of applause.

Beside Spark, Cora leaned forward and spoke into her mic. "Beyond that, the fight mechanics and battle sequences are amazing. Don't be surprised if you come away feeling a bit bruised."

"Figuratively speaking," Mr. Chon said, frowning at Cora. "Of course, there's no actual pain or injury involved. Only a light simulation in the neural interface."

Unless the gamer somehow slipped into the Realm of Faerie. Spark hadn't experienced carry-over, beyond a few scrapes, but both Tam and Jennet had sustained injuries in-game that had been serious in the real world, too.

"So we can't lose weight by playing Feyland?" some joker called out.

"The technology isn't to that point yet," Mr. Chon said.

"But who knows what the future holds? Roc, would you like to add your viewpoint on the game?"

"Sure." Roc pulled his mic closer. "Unlike the girls, I think it's important to note the variety of heroic quests and the depth of the world-building in Feyland. It's not all about feeling the wind on your face."

His sister glared at him, and Spark was torn between annoyance at the put-down and amusement that he'd also insulted Cora.

"Speaking of world-building," the moderator said, "Wilo Martinez and his team put a lot into designing the terrain and features of Feyland. Wilo, what were some of the challenges you faced?"

The panel veered off into a discussion of tech and spec, with Cora interjecting off-topic comments and Roc leaning back, an amused smirk on his face.

Spark answered another question from the moderator, and this time Cora didn't try to hijack the answer. Still, the current of animosity flowing from the twins was so electric she half expected to get a shock when she reached for her water bottle.

"What's next for the intrepid VirtuMax team?" the moderator asked as their time wound to a close.

"I'm pleased to announce the Terabins will be joining Spark in helping debut the FullD system," Mr. Chon said. "A full schedule of their appearances is posted on the events section of our site. This is a historic launch, and VirtuMax is committed to making it fantastic!"

Terrible indeed. Spark forced herself to keep smiling,

though her insides churned. Touring with the Terabins was going to be a nightmare.

The moderator thanked everyone and the crowd applauded. The instant Mr. Chon got up, Spark pushed back her chair and stood. She took a deep breath, but her relief was short-lived as Mr. Chon beckoned her and the Terabins to the front of the stage.

"The press wants some pictures of our top gamers," he said. Glancing at her, he shook his head. "Unfortunate that you're not in uniform, Miss Jaxley."

"Maybe you should dock her pay," Roc said. "Obviously she's not taking this launch as seriously as she should."

"Yeah," Cora said. "Are you sure you've got the right spokesperson for the FullD?"

"Yes," Mr. Chon said. "And all three of you are representing VirtuMax equally. Is that clear?"

"Well, she—" Cora began.

"Fine," Spark said. "I'll wear my costume from now on."

"Smile, everyone," Mr. Chon said.

"Could the gamers bunch together?" one of the reporters called.

Spark edged closer to Roc.

"Miss Jaxley in the middle, please," another photographer said.

"Come on, Fizzle," Cora said, too softly for Mr. Chon to overhear.

She snagged Spark's arm, fingers too tight, and hauled her to stand sandwiched between them. Roc draped his arm over Spark's shoulders and the two Terabins, big smiles on their faces, pressed close, squeezing her until she could barely breathe. Flashes went off, leaving starry afterimages on Spark's retinas. She put on her best photo face, enduring until she couldn't take it any more.

Ducking backwards out of the Terabins' false embrace, she turned to Mr. Chon.

"I need to finish getting my things together," she said.

He nodded, frowning slightly. As she walked away, she could hear Roc say it was too bad she wasn't a team player.

Damn them. Her throat tight, Spark moved to the stairs at the end of the stage. She still had to get through the banquet room without revealing a hint of how disturbed she was that the Terabins were back in her life.

Joe and Burt, ever the loyal guards, flanked Spark as she stepped down. Her fans surged toward her, and she felt the usual twinge of panic, as though one day she might be completely overwhelmed, trampled beneath hundreds of adoring feet.

But not today.

Spark headed for the exit, shaking hands and thanking people. It had taken a while for her to perfect the move where she stuck her hand out just in time to prevent an unwanted hug. Burt had helped her, after she'd been glommed on once too often by an overeager fan. Nothing like getting pressed into the pits of an excited guy who wanted to crush her life essence into his body. Or being clung to by a girl who didn't want to let go so much that her long fingernails left scratches on Spark's arms. So, no hugs.

She did her best to meet her fans' eyes, to look at every person, to put all of her thanks and appreciation into her smile. Still, the faces tended to blur—until one set of features came into sharp focus. Aran. His dark eyes met hers, and held.

Without meaning to, she veered toward him.

"Hey," he said, giving her a half smile.

"Hi." She hadn't expected to see him again, and her breath caught in her throat.

Whatever their connection, it was real. The people around them faded into the background. Though her fans were probably going to gossip like crazy, it didn't matter.

Aran held out his hand, and she took it, his grip warm and firm.

"Since you couldn't make it to the beach," he said, pressing something hard and oval into her palm, "I brought part of it to you."

She looked down, to see a pinkish stone. It was a small thing—and it meant more than she could say.

"It's an agate," he said. "If you get it wet, it's pretty."

"Thanks. For thinking of me."

She wished she could find other words. But there was only goodbye. She closed her hand around the stone; a bittersweet memory, but better than nothing.

He dropped his gaze. "Anyway. Good luck, Spark."

"You too." She stepped forward and hugged him.

After a startled second, Aran's arms came around her, sure and solid, erasing the residue of the Terabins' touch.

Then Burt cleared his throat, Aran let go, and the crowd of fans surrounded her again.

"Goodbye," she said, so quietly he probably didn't hear.

He lifted his hand, and then she lost sight of him as Burt and Joe steered her toward the VIP exit.

"Time's up," Burt called to the crowd. "Head down the road to the Burkesville Mega-Gamma Center tomorrow, the next stop on Spark's tour. See you there!"

She made herself smile and wave at the fans until the door closed behind her. But her other hand was tightly clenched around a small, pink stone.

The redcap goblin, along with two of his kin, bowed low before the midnight throne.

"Has the hour come for us to depart, my lady?" he asked.

The Dark Queen leaned forward. Her pale hands flexed, fingernails biting into the tangled vines. Her smile glittered, sharp as shattered diamonds.

"Yes," she said.

The sibilant word echoed through the clearing. Moon-colored moths fluttered up, startled, only to be caught and devoured by stealthy, dark-winged bats. The court musicians played a low, sorrowful melody, and the night breeze stirred the shadowed oak leaves.

"The mortal moon wanes to darkness," the queen said. "Step aside, Codcadden, and I shall open a portal."

She drew a sharp black thorn from her robes, then gestured to one of the faerie handmaidens beside her throne. Eyes dark with knowledge, the maiden came and knelt before her ruler. The Dark Queen gently cupped her handmaiden's cheek, a world's wealth of sorrow in her face. Then, without a word, she took her thorn and plunged it into the maiden's heart.

A single drop of blood fell upon the velvet-green moss. Silver light emanated upward from the spot, forming an unearthly, radiant ball. The faerie maiden breathed a last sigh and folded like a torn cobweb.

"Make haste," the Dark Queen said to the goblins. "Fetch me the boy 'ere the new dawn wakes, and breaks this dearly won enchantment."

"Yes, my queen," Codcadden said.

He carried a worn leather sack, and his evil smile matched the fierce knives strapped to his belt. Roughly, he pushed his companions into the glowing sphere, leaped in after them, and was gone.

CHAPTER NINE

ARAN DIDN'T BOTHER GOING to sleep. He sat on the lumpy sofa, the blue flicker of his tablet the only light in the Chowneys' garage. Too much soda surged through his system to relax, so he was wasting time following links to all Spark's appearances. Not that he'd show up at any of them, but there was something strangely comforting about knowing where she'd be over the next couple weeks.

The VirtuMax tour would spend a few more days in the area, then head all over the country, basically. Which would be cool, if she had the time—or freedom—to actually visit the cities she appeared in. Too bad she'd missed seeing his hometown.

At least she had a rock as a souvenir.

A rock. Aran shook his head. What had he even been thinking? At the time, it seemed like a romantic gesture, but in hindsight he was embarrassed. *I have a prime crush on you, so here's a stone I picked up.* Weak. It was probably in the bottom of the hotel's trashcan by now.

Enough Spark obsessing. He flicked his tablet to one of his favorite music streams, turned up the earpods, and let the heavy beat and electric guitars anesthetize his brain. Despite the caffeine and sugar pumping through him, his eyes closed, weariness weighting his bones.

Silence, and the feeling of being watched, woke him. With a yawn, he glanced at his tablet. Midnight, exactly, and for some reason his music had cut off. But that wasn't all.

An eerie glow was forming in the middle of the garage. It looked like a digital special effect—a pulsating ball of light that expanded until it was about four feet high. *What the hell?* Aran stood and pulled his earpods out, ready to sprint for the door.

A strand of melody threaded through the air, haunting and melancholy. Then three figures stepped out of the light: three squat creatures, one of which looked familiar. Shock froze Aran's feet, and sped his breath.

No. Way. The goblin from Feyland had not just materialized on the stained concrete floor of the Chowney's old garage.

Except that it had.

"Greetings, Eron. We have come for you, as promised." The goblin held up a worn leather sack and smiled, sharp-toothed and malicious.

"I'm dreaming," Aran said, the words dry in his mouth. He swallowed, and tried again. "I'm not awake. This isn't happening."

The goblin let out a snort. "Foolish mortal. Do you think to bargain with the fey folk and emerge unscathed? Nay, you promised to meet us at midnight on the new moon. The appointed hour has come."

A rank, feral scent filled the garage, like skunk spray. That, more than anything, convinced Aran this was really happening, no matter how surreal. He never smelled stuff in his dreams.

"You're taking me away with you?" His mind scrambled furiously for a way out. Stall the creatures, lull them into thinking he was cooperating, then run.

"Did you not wish to see beyond the scrim of Feyland, to the deeper realm?" the head goblin asked. Behind him, the other two waited, their eyes gleaming.

"I thought..."

What *had* he thought? That the next time he played the game, the system override codes would have something to do with the words "midnight" and "dark moon."

Not that goblins would show up out of a glowing portal.

His heart thumped loudly in his chest. *It's real. It's real.* He took a ragged breath, trying to think.

"Come." The goblin stepped forward, swinging his sack. "'Tis past time to depart."

"Wait!" Aran held up his hands. "I need a minute."

He glanced around the dingy garage. What did he have here? Nothing worth anything, except his friendship with Bix. No cash, no prospects.

And the goblins weren't trying to kill him, though they weren't exactly friendly. He didn't trust them, but something was happening, something big.

Something magic.

Why not go with the creatures? The thought shivered

ANTHEA SHARP

through him, and with it the memory of the boy he'd once been, who had believed. Magic was real, and he had a chance to experience it firsthand.

He snatched up his tablet and opened the messager, quickly keying in the words.

:Bix, I'm going away for a bit. No worries. See you when.:

Vague yet reassuring. He sent the message, then powered off the tablet. No telling what the glowing portal would do to the electronics, but he was taking it along, wherever they were going.

Fear and excitement clogged his throat. Where *were* they going?

"All right," he said to the goblin.

The creature smiled and opened the mouth of the sack wide. A moment later, Aran was engulfed in darkness and foul-smelling leather. He lost his balance, and somehow ended up on his back, completely enclosed by the bag.

"Hey!" he yelled. "Let me out!"

"You must pass between the realms ensconced within the sack," the head goblin said. "Else your mortal senses will be addled beyond use."

The goblin grunted and lifted the bag, making Aran's stomach lurch. Bright light flared around him and the queasiness intensified. He gulped for air, refusing to be sick all over himself.

He was set down with a thump on a springy surface and, to his relief, the goblin opened the sack. Crisp night air, scented with spice and smoke, filled Aran's lungs. A dark sky spread overhead, studded with stars brighter than he'd ever seen.

"My lady," the goblin said. "We have returned with the mortal."

"Unharmed?" The voice was silver and starlight.

"Yes," the goblin said. "As you can see."

His clawed fingers closed around Aran's elbow, hauling him to his knees. Aran blinked as a wave of dizziness and wonder washed over him. He was in a clearing encircled by dark trees. Grotesque and beautiful creatures surrounded him, but they faded to insignificance when he looked up and saw *her*.

His breath caught, lungs aching as though he'd inhaled freezing air. A figure sat before him on a throne made of twisted leaves and vines. She was mystery and enchantment and yearning all rolled into one—but she wasn't human. Her eyes, brilliant and dark, ensnared him with promises, and he was falling…

No. Aran yanked his gaze away, pulse pounding. He didn't know where he was, or even why, but he was not going to lose himself. Not without a fight.

She laughed, a sound that sliced him to the heart.

"Welcome," she said, "to the Dark Court of the Realm of Faerie."

The what? He shot a glance at the knobbled and glimmering creatures arrayed about him. Those scary, dangerous things couldn't possibly be fairies. They weren't cute little flower-dressed pixies with sparkly wings and wide eyes.

"Are you sure?" he asked, keeping his head bent so he wouldn't meet her eyes.

The goblin's claws dug into his skin, so hard Aran felt the blood rise.

"You will address the queen as befits her power and title, mortal," the creature hissed. "You are nothing but dirt beneath her feet."

"Calm yourself, Codcadden," the queen said. "Our guest knows little of our ways, or our realm. He will learn."

There was threat and promise in those words, and Aran shivered. He yanked his arm out of Codcadden's grasp, gritting his teeth as the goblin's claws left streaks of blood on his skin.

A man stepped out from behind the throne, and Aran felt his eyes widen. Not only did the guy look human—in marked contrast to all the other creatures in the clearing—he had a battered guitar slung across his back. His hair was brown, shot through with silver, and he regarded Aran for a long moment, his gaze both wise and weary.

"My lady," the man said, turning to the queen. "I beg leave to counsel and guide this mortal in the ways of the Dark Court."

The queen leaned forward, her dress swirling about her like inky mist. "Betray me not, Bard Thomas. You yet remain overly fond of the human world."

"I am true to you, my queen." The man, Thomas, bowed low. "Did I not prove my worth with the stolen child?"

Aran risked a glance at the queen's face. Her eyes were narrowed and glittering.

"Do not let this human wreak such havoc upon our court as the child did," she said. "Truly I might have reconsidered, had I known the mischief that boy could cause."

Thomas's mouth twitched, as though he held back a smile. Aran made another quick surveillance of the court from beneath his lowered lids. No one else looked even remotely human, so whoever this crazy boy had been, he was gone.

Gone *where* was another question entirely, and one Aran wasn't ready to think about.

"I shall stand responsible for this boy," Thomas said.

"I'm not a child," Aran said, then shut up when the man sent him a sharp look.

"Very well," the queen said. "I give him into your keeping, Bard Thomas. For now. Bring him before me again on the morrow."

"I shall, my lady."

Thomas swept her an elaborate bow, complete with a cloak flourish that should have looked foolish, but instead conveyed a high degree of respect. He stepped over to where Aran knelt, never quite turning his back to the queen, and held out a hand.

"I'm Thomas," he said.

"I gathered that." Aran looked at the man's outstretched hand. He really wanted to refuse any help, but his head was still spinning.

"Come," Thomas said. "It is best not to linger in the queen's sight, once your business with her has concluded."

"Right."

Aran took Thomas's hand. It was warm, his grasp surprisingly firm as he drew Aran to his feet. The scratches on Aran's arm stung, and he glanced down at the bare skin, surprised to see he still had his tablet tucked under his arm. No guarantee it worked here, though. Wherever *here* was.

"You may share my quarters, for now." Thomas let go of

his hand, then turned and led him away from the clearing into the shelter of the trees.

"Somehow, I don't think you have a nice two-story house back in the woods," Aran said.

He glanced around at the moon-silvered forest. The violet flicker of a weird bonfire lit the edges of the clearing, and figures capered there. After a moment of watching the creatures moving on oddly jointed limbs, the flapping of gossamer wings, the waving of too-long fingers, he looked away. He wasn't sure he was ready to deal with this.

"Not quite a house, no." Thomas's voice held a touch of dry humor. "Yet it is a home all the same."

They followed a twisty path a short distance, to a pole with a single, ornate lantern suspended on it. The interior was lit with dancing balls of light. When Aran squinted, he could make out tiny, winged figures inside each glow. They fluttered back and forth, pressing their hands and faces to the sides of the lantern, their mouths open in silent screams. Trapped.

His throat closed, and for a sick moment he couldn't breathe.

"Easy." Thomas was beside him, one hand on his shoulder. "Do not dwell overmuch on the sights here. The Dark Realm is what it is—and not meant for mortals."

Aran swallowed hard. Once. Twice.

"But you live here, and you're mortal." He forced the words out, pretending normalcy despite the fear burning in his lungs.

A sad, tired smile crossed Thomas's lips. "I was mortal, once. Now I belong fully to the realm."

A story there—but Aran didn't want to hear it. Not now.

And clearly Thomas didn't want to tell it, for he started down the path again. Aran caught up with him, and soon he saw a pale blur ahead, between the dark tree trunks.

It was a tent, softly lit with silver radiance, and easily big enough to house ten men. Three peaks rose, the highest in the middle, and from it a flag hung. It was hard to tell in the dim light, but it looked like it depicted a golden harp.

"What did she call you?" he asked. "Not sir or lord…"

"Bard," Thomas said. "I am the Dark Queen's Bard, and my music is sworn to her service. As am I."

Aran didn't ask what that meant. Or think about whether he'd have to do the same. The prickle all down his spine was answer enough. What the hell had he done, coming here?

He shoved the question away and followed Thomas into the tent. Softness cushioned his steps, and he let out a breath at the warmth and color inside. Lanterns—regular ones, lit by candle flame instead of trapped fairies—hung from the ceiling, illuminating the patterned carpets underfoot, the shelves of books, the row of polished instruments Aran couldn't identify.

"Lute, nyckelharpa, hurdy-gurdy, pipes," Thomas said. "Also three guitars, two harps, and an assortment of flutes and whistles. No fiddles, alas."

"You take this bard stuff seriously."

"It is who I am. Have you a passing acquaintance with any musical instrument?"

Aran shrugged. "I played electric bass for a few months, when I was twelve."

"A pity." Thomas lifted one shoulder, then went to one side of the tent and pulled back a crimson hanging.

"My spare room, such as it is," he said. "You are welcome to it."

Aran ducked under the hanging and made a quick survey of the place. Three lanterns hung about the room, and it was cozy, in an otherworldly way. A carpet with blue and green flowers spread across the canvas floor, and in the center of the small room stood a tent pole made of a smooth, living tree. It supported the roof with four branches, and at the peak Aran glimpsed a patch of sky. On one side of the room was a low bed covered with patchwork velvet, and on the other sat a table with curly legs and a top made out of a gigantic leaf. A leaf-like chair was drawn up to the table.

He set his tablet on the table. It looked incongruous—all sleek plas-metal and black glass against the burnished autumn leaf. Later, after Thomas left, he'd see if he could get it working.

The little room had no windows, and he felt his throat tighten again. *Ease off*, he told himself. He could probably yank up the side of the tent and get out that way. Maybe climb the tree and escape overhead—or get his hands on a knife and slash an exit.

Yeah, having a knife would be good, no matter what. Some of the creatures out there had looked severely unfriendly.

He put his hands on hips and turned to face Thomas, who still stood in the doorway.

"How long am I going to be here?" Aran asked.

Inside him a cold wind blew, shredding everything solid he'd ever believed in. Things like the permanence of the world, and the fact that magic didn't, couldn't possibly, exist.

He felt young and old at the same time. As a kid, he'd

buried himself in books about wizards and elves, then moved to the immersive world of sim gaming, fiercely wanting to believe that enchantments were real. He'd finally let go of those dreams. And now here he was, surrounded by the magic he'd finally given up yearning for.

The look in Thomas's eyes started to make sense to Aran, and he pushed back the panic hovering at the edges of his mind. One thing at a time.

"Well." Thomas tilted his head. "How long you remain here depends on you."

"Really? Then why do I feel like I don't have a choice?"

Thomas let out a long sigh. "You chose to come here, did you not?"

"I..."

There were a million excuses Aran could make about not understanding what he'd been getting into, but ultimately, Thomas was right. He had come of his own free will—despite the evidence that things were getting tweaked.

"Yeah," he finally said.

"I wonder why." Thomas's voice was casual, but Aran could hear the steel beneath.

"You know what," Aran said, dropping down to sit on the bed, "I'm pretty wiped. It's a lot to take in."

It was true. The moment he said the words, exhaustion washed over him like a rogue wave, swamping his senses. His head spun, trying to process what had happened.

"Indeed."

Thomas snapped his fingers once, twice, and two of the lanterns dimmed and went out, leaving a soft, nearly colorless darkness behind. The single remaining lamp was a pinprick of light, and the opening at the peak of the roof was suddenly strewn with stars.

"When you are ready," Thomas said, "simply snap to extinguish the final lantern. I bid you good night."

"Night."

Aran bent to unlace his black high-tops, and when he looked up again Thomas was gone. The crimson cloth hung down, a thin barrier between him and the rest of the tent.

Curious, he reached for his tablet and pressed the power button. Nothing. He tried again, but the screen stayed blank and dark. If tech didn't function in the faerie realm, how was he going to figure out Feyland's code?

For a second Aran's lungs squeezed tight, panic thumping through him. What had he agreed to, and where the hell was he?

The soft plunk of guitar strings drifted from the main room of the tent, and slowly his breathing eased. Later. He'd figure it all out later. His head was spinning and sleep was gnawing at his ankles. Tomorrow things would make more sense.

He slid under the covers into a bed soft as thistledown, then snapped off the light. Overhead, the stars brightened. They formed patterns he had never seen, their light clear and remote, and worlds away from home.

CHAPTER TEN

THE VIRTUMAX TOUR bus swooshed down the road, the grav technology hovering it smoothly above the pavement. Spark stared out the window at the winter-bare trees, trying to ignore Roc and Cora, who sat near the front. Although she didn't like riding in the back, it was better than having those two behind her.

"Yo." Vonda leaned forward from the seat across the aisle and waved her hand in front of Spark's face. "Wake up. We'll be at the next venue in a couple minutes."

"I'm here." Spark rubbed her eyes.

She'd let herself forget how monotonous ground tours were. And, truthfully, she'd enjoyed staying in one place for a while, even if that place had been the backwater town of Crestview.

She glanced at the itinerary glowing on her tablet screen. "The game center demo. Why is this marked as a special event?"

"One more gamer is joining the tour," Vonda said. "Virtu-Max's newest superkid."

"Niteesh will be there?" It was the first thing that had made her smile all day.

At last year's international simming tournament, a scrappy eleven-year-old orphan from the New Delhi slums had blasted through the competition and landed straight in the top-ten finalist ring. In addition to his gaming skills, his unfailing good cheer had endeared him to everyone. Well, almost everyone.

Her smile faded as she heard Cora's shrill laughter drift back. The Terabins had given her a rough time, but she hadn't been a kid. Niteesh Singh was streetwise, but he was small for his age. While Spark didn't doubt he could fight dirty if needed, the Terabins had size and strength on their side.

Vonda caught the direction of her gaze.

"Don't worry," she said softly. "We'll be keeping an eye out. Everyone on your team, even if they weren't here at the time, knows about the... incident."

"It won't be enough. Those two are tricky—and dangerous. They don't want any competition. And I mean that in a permanent way."

Vonda shook her head. "There's no proof they were trying to do lasting harm. It was a prank."

"Right."

A few people knew it had been more serious than that, but charges of attempted murder wouldn't look pretty on Virtu-Max's corporate resume.

"It's a temporary thing, Spark. You can deal until the Terabins split off for their own venues."

"It's not me I'm worried about." Well, only a little. She was more concerned for Niteesh. "How long is temporary, in VirtuMax speak?"

Vonda looked at her tablet. "A couple weeks. Until the FullD launch promo winds up."

"All right—but you and the guys better pay attention."

"We will." Vonda's expression was serious. "All of Virtu-Max's gamers are important."

Important, right. To the corporate bottom line.

"After this," Spark said, "I'm going to visit my family."

At least she knew they loved her, even though, since becoming VirtuMax's sim star, her life had changed in ways they couldn't understand. They tried—at least, her parents did, though they could only support her at a distance, seeing as how Mom did all the caretaking for Nana and Papa. Dad couldn't leave his business, and Spark's brother was off at university, doing his own thing. Her younger sister treated her with awe, until she forgot and went back to her usual annoying self.

Mom and Dad were also a little confused by her success. When she'd won the national sim tournament at age fifteen, they'd helped her raise the money to get to the international competition. Once there, she'd scorched her opponents and secured the VirtuMax sponsorship. It had taken some work to bring her parents around, but the salary the company offered, plus the promise of private tutoring to keep her academics up, was ultimately something they couldn't refuse.

She hadn't known then how unglamorous parts of her new life would be, but when her contract came up for renewal, she'd talked her parents into agreeing to one more term. They needed the money. University wasn't cheap, even at the local schools, and Spark was determined that all three kids in her family—herself included—would get the chances her parents never had. Chances none of them would've had, except for her gaming skills.

The bus slowed, the plas-metal and concrete building of the gaming center coming into view. Spark glanced at the long line snaking around the corner. A bunch of national vid crews were there, too, judging from the number of satellite-topped vans parked beside the gaming center. SimCon might have been the first demo, but this event had obviously been built up as something splashy.

"I'm going to change," she said as soon as the bus stopped.

The back part of the vehicle was a deluxe bathroom, complete with a closet and changing room. Spark pulled out her teal-blue costume, then froze in disbelief. A long rip gaped in the fabric in back, running from the plastic shoulder guards down to the built-in belt.

Dammit! She should have been paying better attention to the Terabins' movements—but she hadn't thought far enough ahead. Of course they'd try to sabotage her. Clearly their new tactic was to discredit her, make it seem as though she didn't take her position seriously.

The problem was, the twins were right. Being VirtuMax's sim star wasn't that important, not compared to her new job as a guardian of the border between human and fey worlds. But that was hardly something she could explain.

Even though being a Feyguard was huge, so far she was still clueless about what it entailed. Whereas her job as Spark

Jaxley, helping launch the FullD system, was immediate and pressing.

And she had nothing to wear. She rifled through the rest of her clothing, but her other two Spark suits were also damaged beyond use. One had a big purple stain on it, and the other one's chest plate was scraped up. Boy, the twins didn't mess around, but they'd done it in a way that wasn't obvious. Her word against theirs, and with the mood Mr. Chon had been in, she didn't like her chances.

Spark held up her ruined blue costume. She had to figure out how to salvage this.

"Vonda?" she called, sticking her head out of the bathroom.

The Terabins noticed, and Cora let out a snicker. Spark ignored them.

"Yeah?" Vonda came over. "What's going on?"

"Wardrobe malfunction." Spark kept her voice low. "Could you get me some duct tape?"

"Got a roll in my bag. One sec."

Vonda did a good job of getting the silver duct tape out of her bag and tucking it under her shirt. The twins scowled, but they couldn't quite see what was happening.

"Here." Vonda handed her the roll. "Anything else?"

"I got it, for now. If you can get some other gaming costumes together for me, though, that would be good."

Spark shut the door on her manager's concerned expression and set to work. She taped up the rip in the back of the teal suit, then wriggled into it. The fabric pulled oddly, and she made a few more adjustments to the back. It wasn't pretty, nor comfortable, but she could deal with that.

One of her other costumes had a short cloak. It was lemon yellow—not the smoothest color combo with teal—but it would cover up the mess on her back. Spark slung it on, then grabbed the yellow belt, too.

Adequately dressed, she rummaged through her makeup. At least her cosmetics were untouched, though from now on she was locking everything up. She'd have to ask Vonda for some secure containers.

Spark did her usual stage makeup, then added a few swipes of bright color to her eyelids—yellow and teal, to try and pull her look together. It wasn't a perfect success, but at least she wouldn't be showing up on the national gaming news in a T-shirt. Which had clearly been the Terabins' aim.

Her mangled yellow suit was decorated with shiny crystals at the neck. Spark pried a few off and glued them down one cheek. Might as well go for the full-on treatment.

Vonda rapped at the bathroom door. "Ready?"

"As ready as I can be." Spark stepped out. "Don't say anything."

She glanced up the length of the bus, glad to see the twins had already gone. They'd make cutting remarks when they saw her. Not too many, though. Not in public.

"Right." Vonda blinked at her, then turned back to the door. "I'll just lock this."

When Spark exited the bus, the crowd cheered. Vid cams slewed around to get footage of her. Holding her chin high, she waved and smiled, then let Vonda lead her to the employees' entrance. She hoped none of the duct tape showed from behind.

Burt waited just outside the door, ready to bounce

anybody that tried to sneak in. He nodded at her and didn't seem to notice she was oddly dressed. Of course, the gamer costumes were varying degrees of strange and flashy. She could pull this off, as long as she acted confident. The trick was not to let the twins rattle her.

Burt pulled open the door, and she and Vonda stepped into a drab room holding a couple of couches, a table with a coffeemaker, and a hand-lettered sign that read *Welcome, VirtuMax gamers!*

The Terabins looked up from where they sat on one of the gray couches, paper cups of coffee in their hands. Roc laughed. A second later Cora did, too, but the look on her face wasn't amusement. That, more than anything, let Spark know her suit mash-up actually worked. The knowledge warmed her. So much for their little plan.

"Sparky!"

A boy dressed in bright orange and red sprang up to wrap his wiry arms around her middle.

"Niteesh." She returned his hug. "Good to see you. And you're the only one allowed to call me that, remember?"

He grinned at her, his dark eyes sparkling in his brown face, and stepped back. "Oh, sure. How was SimCon?"

"Good." For a second, Aran's face hovered in her mind. "Nothing extra-prime, though. Glad you're joining the tour."

"I'd have come to the con, too, except for the underage work laws." Niteesh snorted. "Man, they should see how the kids work in India."

"You're in the civilized world now," Cora said. "I know it's hard. Get used to it."

Niteesh ignored the comment, like the smart kid he was.

"What do you think of Feyland?" Spark asked him.

"Good." Niteesh gave a single, sharp nod. "A little predictable, but what can you do?"

Spark let out a breath she didn't realize she'd been holding. The Feyland that connected to the Realm of Faerie was highly unpredictable, which meant that, so far, Niteesh was safe.

"Maybe you should get into game design." She smiled at him.

It wouldn't surprise her if at some point he invented a radically new game concept. One of the things that made Niteesh a top simmer—in addition to light-speed reflexes—was his ability to come up with weirdly creative approaches to in-game problems.

"Doors are opening," Vonda announced. "You all ready?"

Roc and Cora got up from the couch, and Niteesh nodded, his curly black hair bouncing. As the four gamers entered the main room of the gaming center, the crowd applauded and yelled. Lights rigged for the event strobed wildly, overpowering the daylight filtering through the tinted glass windows.

Spark followed Niteesh to where the FullD systems stood. Four of them were arranged behind velvet ropes, each one hooked to the overhead monitor display.

"Our special guests need no introduction," the game center manager announced with a bleached-bright smile.

He then proceeded to introduce them, and Niteesh rolled his eyes at Spark. After a rambling introduction, followed by an explanation of how customers should pick up their pre-ordered FullD systems, the manager waved his hand.

"Let's get to the fun!" he cried.

Vonda nodded confirmation, and the VirtuMax gamers pulled on helmets and gloves, then slipped into their sim chairs. Spark's was the same system she'd played on at SimCon —polished up and custom painted to match her hair. Niteesh had flames scribed on the side of his, and Roc and Cora's setups were blue-black, decorated with white bursts of light.

Spark gave the command to enter game, and the outside world disappeared. She stood in the usual clearing surrounded by tall trees. The moss felt soft as a plush carpet beneath her feet, and a faerie ring enclosed her; the mushrooms a mix of pale, moon-colored ones and bright red ones spotted with white. She let herself relax into the chair a little more. The faerie ring was usually the first indicator that things were getting tweaked. So far, so normal.

The other avatars materialized around her. She wasn't surprised to see Roc geared up as an Assassin, and Cora in the robes of a Spellcaster. Niteesh wore full Warrior armor, and carried a huge sword that was probably bigger than he was in real life.

He'd told her he always liked to play big, bulky characters. Not to make up for being small, but for the surprise factor against other gamers. His trick, though, was that he stacked nimbleness and agility on his avatar profiles whenever possible, so he still moved fast despite playing heavily armored classes.

"Make room," Roc said. "I think it's time to demonstrate the PVP abilities in here."

Of course the Terabins would go directly to player-versus-player combat. Spark should have anticipated it.

"I challenge you, warrior boy." Cora pointed her mage staff at Niteesh.

"Accepted," he said, bringing up his shield just in time to deflect a blast of arcane light.

"Well?" Roc said. "Think your fox-girl has what it takes?"

Before she even spoke the words to accept the challenge, Roc vanished. No doubt he was sneaking behind her, trying to go for a killing blow.

She threw herself flat, then rolled. A blade swished harmlessly through the air where she'd just been, and Roc reappeared, scowling. She flung her boot dagger at him, but his reflexes were too good and he slid out of the way, the blade missing.

It was going to be a good fight, and she grinned at the challenge. Out of the corner of her eye, she saw a fireball fly across the clearing. Niteesh's sword flashed and Cora muttered a curse. Spark hoped Vonda was taking notes; VirtuMax gamers weren't supposed to swear while playing in public, no matter how hot things got.

Roc, however, was always in control, which made Spark's job harder. She wouldn't be able to goad him into making a stupid move out of anger.

"So, you want to play with knives?" Two wickedly sharp blades appeared in his hands.

He spun into a blur of motion, and Spark backed up. Although her Kitsune wasn't best equipped for hand-to-hand, she had a few tricks. She called up the power of air, conjuring a solid wall that stopped Roc in his tracks. In the second it took him to regroup, she dropped the air wall and sent a spear of fire at him.

Roc hissed in surprise and brought his knives up in a classic block, deflecting the burning tip. It nicked his upper arm and the air flashed yellow, signaling he'd taken a hit.

Not enough of one to count as victory, though. The elements weren't easy to manipulate, and her attack had taken all her magical strength for the moment. She danced back, grabbed her bow, and nocked an arrow. Roc had gone invisible again. Not good.

The whisper of cloth behind her was her only warning. She dodged to the side, but Roc had anticipated her move. His blade slid around to hover across her throat, a kiss of cold metal waiting to bite.

"Surrender?" he asked.

Realization flashed through her. Roc didn't want to just win this, he wanted to humiliate her in front of the audience. He thought he had her defeated. Too bad for him.

"Never," she said.

An instant later, she was a fox, her perspective flattened and low, washed of color. She dug her four paws into the ground and dashed between Cora and Niteesh, narrowly avoiding being scorched by an arcane bolt. In another heartbeat, she whirled and returned to her human form—still carrying her bow.

Roc rounded the other fighters, but she'd gained precious time and distance. Spark let her arrow fly, fast and true. It struck Roc in the chest, and he fell to his knees. Her visor screen lit up with a green flash. Victory!

"Bah." Roc stood and brushed off his black leather vest, though the arrow had disappeared the moment it hit. Unlike actual combat, the loser of a duel didn't die, just had their character frozen for a few seconds.

"Winner!" Niteesh called out, a note of glee in his voice.

Spark glanced over to see him sheathing his sword, while Cora scowled.

"You got a lucky hit in," she said. "Next time, you're dust."

"Oh, sure." Niteesh laughed. "Come on, guys. We have a game to show off."

"Please do." Vonda's voice sounded over their headsets. "Although folks appreciated the PVP demonstration."

Without waiting for the rest of them, Roc jumped over the mushroom boundary and headed down the path winding between the white-trunked trees. Spark took a step forward, wanting to keep him in sight. A strange buzzing sound filled the air, and sudden static crackled through the scene. Weird.

She took another step, and Feyland rippled and wavered. Niteesh asked her something, the words garbled as though spoken underwater. And then, with a stomach-wrenching lurch, she was *elsewhere*.

Not the simulated world of Feyland, and not the midnight glade of the Dark Court. An eerie landscape stretched around her, a series of flat, purplish plains shading into deep red at the horizon. The sky was evenly lit, a featureless silver bowl clapped down over the ground. Where was she? She turned, heartbeat pounding in her throat. Nothing moved.

"Hello?" she called. "Niteesh? Vonda?"

Silence.

Then a voice came, without sound, the meaning forming in her mind.

Guardian of the balance. You are called.

Oh, crap. She'd wondered how the Elder Fey would communicate with them if the Feyguard were needed. But right now—in the middle of a demo?

She desperately hoped the watching crowd couldn't see her. If they did, there would be way too much explaining to do. She had to trust that the Elder Fey knew what they were doing.

"Called where?" The words were dry in her throat. "What am I supposed to do?"

A mortal has entered the Dark Court. You must free him.

Worry cracked through her. This was it—she'd been called up as a Feyguard and she had no idea what to do. Tam and Jennet were the experts on the Realm of Faerie. She'd only been there once, and the memory still woke her at night, dreams of ice and blackness that left her shivering.

"Free him—by myself? How do I get there?"

The usual way. The voice held dry amusement, and a hint of exasperation, like a parent speaking to a child.

Fair enough, she supposed. If being a Feyguard were easy, everyone would be doing it.

"What am I supposed to—"

Enough. Perform your duties, and do not bestir us again from our dreaming.

"Wait!" She stretched out her hand, though there was nothing to catch.

The purple landscape flared, then dissolved. Spark doubled over, aching as though someone had punched her in the gut. Velvet-green mosses blurred in her vision.

"You okay?" Niteesh's voice was concerned as his hand gripped her elbow.

She swallowed back nausea and straightened. No matter how wretched she felt, she could give no sign that she'd just... what? Been ripped out of reality for a few moments?

"I'm fine."

She darted a look around the clearing. Cora stood outside the circle, watching them impatiently, and Spark could see Roc's figure disappearing through the trees. Apparently only a few heartbeats had passed.

"Your avatar disappeared for a sec," Niteesh said. "It was weird."

"It's nothing." Spark shook her hair back from her face. "Let's go."

Niteesh tipped his head, and she strode past him, unwilling to meet his eyes. The kid was too smart. Even if nobody else suspected anything, he would. Though the truth was so tweaked as to be un-guessable.

Yeah, otherworldly creatures just pulled me into a different dimension, where they put me on the clock and gave me obscure instructions.

The rest of the demo game was a blur. She fought decently, and didn't say much as the four VirtuMax gamers completed a quest series. Roc and Cora seemed happy to hog the spotlight, but Niteesh kept giving her worried looks.

Still, showing off her skills in a simulated game was trivial compared to what had just happened.

She had to get to the Dark Court "the usual way," which meant via Feyland. And clearly she couldn't go jaunting off while in demo. Somehow she'd have to figure out a way to sneak onto the FullD. And she needed to message Jennet and Tam as soon as possible, though she had a sinking feeling they hadn't been called up by the Elder Fey. Still, they'd have some ideas. But it basically came down to one thing.

Someone was trapped in the Realm of Faerie, and it was up to her to rescue them.

CHAPTER ELEVEN

A<small>RAN</small> <small>WOKE</small>, the scent of mint and cinnamon in his nose instead of the musty smell of the Chowney's garage. Above him, the unfamiliar, bright stars shone through the opening in the tent peak. It felt like morning, despite the night sky overhead. He stretched, the covers silky against his skin, then got out of bed.

The plush rug welcomed his bare feet, and the air was warm enough to be comfortable. He pulled on his jeans, then bit back a yelp as something dug painfully into the arch of his left foot. He bent and felt around on the carpet until the hard, ridged object met his fingers. It took a few yanks to get it out of the silky strands of the rug, as if the thing had been cocooned.

Aran held it up, then blinked in disbelief. It was a cheap plastic dragon toy—the kind that came in kid's fast-food meals. The bright orange plastic shone, as garishly out of place as a neon sign in a candlelit dining hall. No question it had come from the mortal world, but how?

The events of yesterday were blurry, but he chased the memory down. Something the Dark Queen had said about a troublesome mortal child. Aran wasn't the first visitor here, and the confirmation of it made the skin between his shoulder blades prickle. What had happened to that kid?

And did he even want to know?

He shrugged on his sweatshirt, suddenly chilled, then slipped the plastic toy into his pocket. It felt good to have a piece of his own world to carry around.

Pulling aside the crimson curtain, he stepped into the main room of the tent. Thomas sat at a table set along one wall, writing with a feather pen on what looked like parchment.

"Good day," Thomas said.

"Is it?"

"An intriguing question." Thomas set his pen down and nodded to an empty wicker chair. "Sit, and we will discuss it."

Aran swung the chair around and sat backwards, resting his arms along the woven willow top. "We have a lot more than that to discuss."

"Indeed. But it is a start. Tea?"

"Sure."

Thomas picked up a green teapot and poured a stream of pale gold liquid into a matching cup. The steam swirling over the surface carried the scents that had woken Aran: cinnamon and mint. He took a careful sip, and the tea spread through his mouth, tasting like a perfect summer day.

"Cake?" Thomas pushed a deep blue plate filled with biscuit-like pastries toward him. "I will, however, caution you

117

to eat no bite nor sip no sup outside the confines of these walls."

The guy had the oddest way of talking, but Aran could follow him. More or less. He reached for one of the cakes.

"Why's that?"

"Let us begin with your initial inquiry." Thomas gave him a thoughtful look. "Is it, indeed, a good day? Firstly, whether goodness favors your mood is entirely up to you. And for the second part, it is not, in fact, day—a detail I commend you for noticing."

"So, when does the sun come up? Does this place run on a super-extended clock or something?"

"In all the time you bide here it will never be day, for this is the Dark Court, where midnight and moonlight hold sway."

Aran wrapped his hands around his teacup, trying to push away the chill brought on by Thomas's words.

"I have a feeling I'm going to miss the sun," he said.

Even though it was winter in the mortal world, at least the sun was *there*—a glowing ball of fire lurking behind the clouds. Endless night was going to get stale pretty quick.

"Of a certainty, you will long for the daylight," Thomas said, his voice laced with old sorrow. "I do."

"So, how'd you get here? And can you ever leave?"

The questions left a sour taste in Aran's mouth, and he took another hasty drink of tea. Was he trapped here, like those tiny fairies in the lanterns, unable to escape?

Escape to what? a cynical voice inside him asked. *No money, a useless attraction to a gamer girl, and every step overshadowed by the black cloud of a criminal record?*

"Answers for answers," Thomas said. "First, we need something to call you by."

"My name's Ar—"

"Stop." Thomas held up his hand. "Names have power here. Is there a name—not your birth-given one—you go by in the mortal world?"

"BlackWing."

It was somehow fitting to claim his hacker identity here. And it wasn't like anyone would recognize it.

"Good." Thomas lifted a cake from the plate. "Mortals who eat or drink in the Realm of Faerie are trapped here. Only the food I serve you is free of that binding enchantment."

Aran studied his cake. He had no reason not to trust Thomas. With a shrug, he took a bite. It was honey-sweet and warm, as if freshly out of the oven. He finished the cake in three bites, then snagged another.

"Is that what happened to you?" he asked. "Ate something you shouldn't have?"

"No."

"Then you could go back, if you wanted?"

Thomas gave a low, weary sigh. "I cannot. There is nothing for me to return to. Tell me, why did the goblins bring you here, to the Dark Queen?"

Aran swallowed the last bite of cake, then took a sip of tea, buying time while he thought. There was plenty he didn't want to say—and plenty he guessed Thomas wasn't telling him, either.

"It sounds strange, but I met the goblin in a computer game."

"Feyland, I suppose?" Something flashed across Thomas's

expression, a momentary easing of the anxious lines in his face.

"Yeah." Aran narrowed his eyes. "How'd you know that?"

"Feyland and the Realm of Faerie are connected."

"That's just... tweaked." Aran set his cup down and folded his arms along the back of the chair. Crazy as it was, though, the evidence was all around him. "Care to tell me how that happened?"

"Another time, perhaps. Your audience with the queen draws nigh. If I am to aid you, I must understand why you are here."

"Yeah, well, I don't quite understand it myself."

He wasn't going to tell Thomas he'd been trying to hack Feyland. He had a feeling the bard wouldn't think too highly of that idea.

Thomas firmed his lips and studied Aran with a look that made him feel like a disobedient child.

"Look." Aran unfolded his arms and stood. "I just want something better out of life. I was given an opportunity, and I took it. I didn't know it would bring me here."

"Do you wish to return to the mortal world?"

"Not at the moment, no. So, what do I need to do to get ready to see the queen?"

He'd take one thing, one minute, at a time. It was the only way to cope when life got complicated. Thinking too much caused a crazy whirlwind in his brain that could suck him under—that *had* sucked him under in the past. Those first few months in juvie had been nothing but panic and fear. It had taken too long for him to get his bearings, to pull himself together, and he was never making that mistake again. Never.

Spark signed autographs and posed for pictures, but the whole time her mind clamored with questions. At last the game center event ended, and she hurried back to the bus. Tucking herself into the back corner seat, she pulled out her messager. First priority was talking to Tam and Jennet.

Tam, as usual, didn't answer, but Jennet responded right away.

:How's the tour going?: she asked.

:Crazy. The Elder Fey contacted me in-game and told me I'm supposed to rescue someone from the Dark Realm.:

:What?!:

:I know. Have you guys been playing Feyland? Did they get in touch with you and Tam?: Spark tried not to hold her breath for the answer.

:We were in-game earlier today. Nothing unusual happened.:

:I don't want to do this alone.: Spark chewed on her lower lip. *:You and Tam are the ones with experience.:*

:Maybe that's why they didn't ask us. The game's releasing now. If we're all helping the same person, who's on call when other people get in trouble?:

Jennet was right, though Spark didn't like it. She'd seen the danger and power of the Dark Queen, but unlike her friends, Spark had never faced her in direct combat. At least, not solo. It had taken seven of them fighting together, plus a powerful talisman, to defeat her last time. Also, Spark's memory of that battle was a little hazy, since she'd been a fox during key moments.

The bus swayed as the rest of the VirtuMax team climbed

on. Niteesh headed toward her, a determined look on his face. He was going to ask her what was going on, and she had no idea what to tell him.

:I gotta go,: she typed.

:Talk again soon,: Jennet replied. *:I'll see what Tam thinks.:*

Spark turned off her messager. Lucky Jennet, to have somebody to share things with.

"Hey," she said as Niteesh took the seat next to her.

"Is for horses," he said. "What's going on with you?"

"Off day. It happens."

"You're a terrible liar." When she didn't reply, he squinched his lips together. "Fine, don't tell me."

"If I could, I would." She hoped he believed her. The last thing she wanted to do was alienate the only friend she had on the tour.

He gazed at her, his eyes bright, then shrugged.

"Whatever. So, what happened to your clothes?"

"What do you think?" Spark shot a look to the front of the bus, where Roc and Cora sprawled, taking up a row of seats each.

"Thought so," Niteesh said. "But I'm here now to watch your back."

"And vice versa. They don't love you any better."

The bus glided into motion, and Spark stared out the window as the parking lot of the gaming center slid away.

"Yeah, but I'm just a little kid," Niteesh said, a note of irony in his voice. "You're the real competition. Keep your edge, though—don't make it easy for them."

Spark let out a sigh that misted the window glass.

"I know, I was distracted in there." By otherworldly creatures giving her cryptic instructions. "In order to focus, I need some more time in-game."

"You need to practice?" He gave her a confused look. "You, Spark Jaxley?"

"Something like that." She leaned forward to make sure Roc and Cora couldn't see her face. It wouldn't surprise her if they read lips. "Think you could help me figure out a way to get secret system time?"

His eyes brightened, and he tapped his lips with one finger. Niteesh was one sneaky kid, and between the two of them, Spark knew they could get her on a FullD. Vonda would probably help, too, although the more people who knew what Spark was up to, the harder it would be to keep secret. And to keep her own secrets about why, exactly, she needed to play Feyland during off hours.

"I got it," Niteesh said. "We'll tell Vonda we have to brush up our PVP skills, since we know the Terabins are going to keep trying to jump us."

"But we both won our duels with them," Spark said. "It's not a good enough excuse."

"Then tell her your interface is glitchy, and that's why you had issues today. Because, I tell you, your play was clearly off."

More lies. She was getting tired of them—but what could she do?

"Okay. I'll go back and talk to Vonda."

"If that doesn't work, we can always break into the FullD trailer late at night, bring an auxiliary power source, and get you going that way." He grinned and flexed his fingers. "I'm good with security codes."

"Too dangerous. I'm sure VirtuMax has serious safeguards

on those systems. Let me talk to Vonda first, before we try anything too crazy."

Though it could come to that. Her "glitchy interface" excuse would only work once, and Spark had a feeling she'd need a couple of sessions in-game to get to the Dark Court.

Jennet had talked a little bit about when she'd first played Feyland. There were several levels the gamer had to complete, each one leading closer and closer to the court, until at last they faced the Dark Queen.

Spark had to win her way to the court and battle the queen in order to free whoever was trapped there. The thought sent a chill down her spine. How much worse was it for the poor gamer who had somehow stumbled into the Realm of Faerie? Even now they could be in terrible danger.

CHAPTER TWELVE

ARAN FOLLOWED Thomas down the dim path leading to the Dark Court. His fingers were cold, and he pulled the thick cloak closer about his shoulders. Not that a fancy new outfit could ease the chill he felt at the thought of standing before the Dark Queen again.

Thomas had come up with an intricate set of clothing for Aran to wear for his audience. The shirt and close-fitting pants were nice and basic, but the tooled leather boots and vest embroidered in indigo and silver were too gaudy for his taste. Still, he didn't argue about putting them on. At least the dark blue cloak covered much of the vest, and he could live with the ornate pin holding it closed at his throat.

Thomas paused at the edge of the court clearing, his figure silhouetted by the eerie violet light of the bonfire.

"Any last-minute advice?" Aran asked. He tried to make the question cocky, though it came out a little scared.

"Speak but few words. The less you say, the less fuel you provide for the queen's anger."

"Right."

At some point, Aran intended to find out why the queen was so mad. So far, Thomas had dodged his questions, claiming it wasn't a good idea to discuss anywhere near the Dark Court.

"Show me your formal bow once again," Thomas said.

"Are you sure it's necessary?"

Although Aran thought of himself as fairly coordinated, the complex court bow Thomas had drilled into him was not an easy move to master.

"Yes." There was no room for argument in Thomas's tone.

With a deep breath, Aran swept back the cloak, then stepped forward onto his right foot. He dipped low, sweeping his right arm out, while his left went behind him for balance. When he started to straighten, Thomas tapped him on the back.

"Hold," he said. "You may not rise until the queen gives you leave."

"My leg is killing me."

"'Tis not a matter for joking, BlackWing. More than your leg will be in pain, should you disrespect the queen."

Aran gritted his teeth and held the position, ignoring the hot jabs of discomfort in his muscles. Yeah, he was a rebel, like Spark had said—but there were times when you played by the rules. Until you knew when, where, and how to break them.

"Rise," Thomas said. "You are ready."

Provided he didn't fall flat on his face. Aran unbent and rocked back onto his heels, easing the tension from his body.

"Ready as I'll be," he said. "Lead on."

As they stepped into the clearing, the babble of fey voices

rose. The figures cavorting in front of the fire paused, watching him with avid gazes. At the far side of the clearing, a tall figure stood, his head crowned with antlers gilded silver by the distant moon. Lithe hounds curled, serpentine, around his feet. There was something incredibly creepy about him, and Aran averted his eyes.

Thomas led him past the banquet tables laid with food he couldn't eat. Not that he'd want to—the silver goblets were filled with a heavy, dark red liquid that looked like blood, and the delicacies glowed with strange colors on their burnished plates.

Sweet, melancholy music twined through the clearing; a breathy flute accompanied by the solemn beat of a drum. The air held the whisper of a chill, more pronounced as they drew closer to the throne. Aran darted a glance at the queen, her terrible, beautiful face framed by hair black as midnight, soft as smoke.

Then they were before the tangled throne. Thomas swept into the court bow, and Aran followed, feeling clumsy. He remained bent over, barely breathing, his heartbeat thumping loudly in his ears.

"Bard Thomas, BlackWing, rise," the queen said at last.

Aran cautiously straightened, careful not to meet her mesmerizing gaze. Instead, he watched the gossamer-winged faerie maidens clustered behind the throne. With their haunted eyes and pale skin, they looked as if they never smiled.

"Stand forward, BlackWing," the queen commanded, "and tell me what you seek in the Realm of Faerie."

Swallowing, he took a step toward the throne. Thomas

stood at his shoulder, and Aran was grateful for the support. Even though they didn't trust one another, Thomas was a decent guy.

"Address her formally," the bard whispered to him as Aran opened his mouth.

Right. He paused a moment, considering what to say.

"Your majesty—I'm here because the goblin told me this is where I'd be able to see what lies behind Feyland. That's what I want."

Beside him, Thomas drew in a sharp breath.

"Are you satisfied with what you have found?" the queen asked, a bite of laughter in her voice.

"Not exactly."

He never would have guessed actual magic underlay the sim game of Feyland. How was a guy supposed to hack that? Learn a bunch of spells? It was ridiculous, in a horrible kind of way.

"You are a mortal skilled in the use of this so-called game and its interface, are you not?"

"I guess." Not that he'd had much of a chance to play Feyland.

The Dark Queen smiled, and Aran blinked at the way the clearing lightened, as if dusted with starlight. Her deep eyes were filled with mystery, and he swayed, dizzy from the force of her expression.

"Steady," Thomas said in an undertone, catching his arm.

Aran yanked his gaze back down to the deep green moss underfoot and pulled in a steadying breath. The queen's laughter sifted over him, light as chiming bells.

"Ah, I forget how easily you mortals are undone," she said.

"I have a challenge for you, BlackWing. I greatly desire to open my realm more fully to the human world—and to do this, I need someone who understands the inner workings of Feyland."

"Wait." Aran blinked. "You want me to hack into the real world from here, using Feyland?"

"Just so." Her voice softened, melting like honey around his senses. "Can you do this thing for me?"

Half of him wanted to say yes to her, yes to anything she asked. But he'd learned caution in the most painful way possible.

"Is that a good idea?" he asked. "For us humans, I mean."

Thomas squeezed his arm, but the queen was clearly displeased by his answer. Eyes glittering like diamonds, she leaned forward. Aran hadn't noticed before how long and deadly looking her fingernails were.

"Do you dare to question me?" Her voice was a cold blade slicing the air.

"My lady," Thomas said. "He is not your subject, to command as you please. And if you recall, he is but newly come to the realm. Forgive him for his brashness."

The queen's eyes narrowed, and she sat back. Aran let out a breath he didn't realize he'd been holding.

"Although I owe you no explanation, mortal," she said, "know that the Realm of Faerie will wither and die if the gate is not opened. And you shall be well rewarded. Wealth and power are within your grasp. Only do this one thing for me."

Aran curled his chilled fingers into his palms. Somehow, he didn't think reverse-hacking his way into the human world was going to be simple. But he also suspected he didn't have a choice.

"What good will wealth and power do me, here?" he asked, glancing to the creatures clustered about the throne. The goblin, Codcadden, grinned, showing his pointed teeth.

Aran didn't want to boss faeries around, plus he didn't think they'd take orders from a human all that well. The things he wanted weren't found in the Realm of Faerie. Or maybe anywhere. He was smart enough to know that most of them couldn't be bought, either.

"The boy speaks truly," Thomas said. "One of his payments must be a return to the mortal realm."

"If he is able to prove himself, he shall reap the rewards," the queen said. "And if not, then you shall have an apprentice, Thomas. Forever."

The finality in her words made Aran's gut turn to ice. This just got worse and worse.

"I'll want payment in gold," he said. "And I'm going to need some gear." Though he had no idea what.

The Dark Queen waved her hand. "Agreed. Bard Thomas shall equip you as necessary. I expect you to succeed in this, mortal boy."

"I will."

Despite having no clue how to accomplish what the queen wanted, failure wasn't an option. Aran looked at Thomas's weary face, the sorrow lying heavy in his eyes.

No way was Aran going to spend eternity trapped in the Realm of Faerie.

"Thanks, Vonda," Spark said as the road crew finished hooking up her FullD system.

It took up most of the space in her hotel room, wedged between the bed and wall, but she wasn't planning on sleeping much, anyway. She had a lot of simming to do.

During their takeout dinner, she'd convinced her manager to let her use the sim system to "work out the glitches" for the upcoming demos. Vonda had given her a funny look, but gave Spark permission to use a FullD for the evening.

"Get your mojo back," Vonda said. "We load out at noon tomorrow. That's all the sim time I can give you."

"How far is it to the next gig?"

"Four hours. You're on for the demo at six tonight, and I want you fresh and on your game, all right?" Vonda pointed at her.

"Yes, ma'am." Spark saluted.

"Don't stay up too late."

"Mhm."

"Good night then." Vonda rolled her eyes as she shut the door, clearly understanding that Spark had made no promises.

Spark threw the deadbolt, checked to make sure the windows were locked and the curtains shut tight, then fired up her system. She didn't relish the thought of an all-night marathon, but she might not get another chance to enter Feyland unobserved.

On the other hand, she couldn't totally stint on sleep, or it would show during the demo appearances. She couldn't afford any more slips, not with the Terabins waiting for her to falter.

One thing at a time. Her first job was to get in-game and help whoever had inadvertently stumbled into the Realm of Faerie.

She put on the helmet and gloves and activated Feyland. At the character screen, she paused. Should she make a new avatar, one better suited to solo questing?

She hovered over the description of the Knight, then shook her head. Straightforward melee fighting had never been her style. Plus she'd already mastered a few of her Kitsune's tricks. Better to play a familiar class. If that didn't work, she could start over with a new character. As if she had time to do that.

Before she could waste more time second-guessing, Spark flicked her fingers in the command to enter game. Spinning golden light enfolded her, and for once she welcomed the queasy sensation. She'd been worried that Feyland wouldn't take her into the realm, but the feeling of transitioning out of the real world was unmistakable.

A moment later, she stood in the familiar sunlit clearing. Everything looked the same, except for one key difference. The mushrooms in the faerie ring encircling her were pale white, the color of moonlight. Proof that she was on the way to the Dark Court.

She checked that her weapons were in place, then strode down the path. The branches of the white-barked trees interlaced above her head, sending a lattice of shadows across the soft moss. Bright orange butterflies flickered in and out of shafts of sunlight, and the whole forest seemed peaceful and serene.

Too bad it was the anteroom to a land filled with evil fey

folk. She had a few levels to go to reach the court, however— at least according to Jennet.

When the bus had arrived at their hotel for the night, Spark had checked in and then messaged Jennet from the privacy of her room. Apparently, when Jennet and Tam had battled the Dark Queen, they'd had to complete a number of very strange quests, progressing through different areas of Feyland until they reached the court. It was the game, but tweaked.

Although there might be a shortcut. Jennet had advised her to keep watch for Puck.

:*That freaky sprite?*: Spark had asked.

:*Yes. He can be very helpful, so watch for him.*:

Spark wasn't so sure. She'd only seen a bit of Puck—both in the real world and the realm. While he'd assisted them a couple times, the main thing she remembered was that he'd ridden her fox form as if she was a horse. Kind of demeaning, to be used as the personal mount of a fey little creature.

Something rustled in the underbrush beside the path. Spark whirled, one hand on her dagger. Nothing appeared. She stood still, trying to breathe silently, and stared at the bushes for a long moment.

"Okay then," she said. "But I know you're there, whatever you are."

There was no answer—and she didn't have time to stand around arguing with shrubbery. Keeping a wary eye out, Spark continued on. So what if her pace increased almost to a run. She was in a hurry.

The trees thinned, and the path led from the forest's edge into a sunny meadow filled with blue and red flowers. A short way along the path stood a cottage right out of an English countryside postcard, complete with a thatched roof and windows mullioned in tiny squares of glass.

The creature squatting on the doorstep, though, definitely detracted from the picture. He was covered in long black hair, his beard tangled with twigs and mosses. The nails of his knobbly toes and crooked hands were grimy and uneven. A whiff of rotting vegetables rose from where he sat, and Spark wrinkled her nose. Ready to leap into combat if necessary, she slowly approached the cottage.

Two beady, malicious eyes regarded her, but the creature made no move to attack.

"Greetings," Spark said, stopping a few feet from the door.

"Fox-girl," the creature said, his voice rough, as though he seldom spoke, "do you seek a quest?"

"I do."

"Heh." The hairy man chewed on the end of his beard a moment. Then he spat it out, and pointed down the path. "Yonder lies the tree of copper apples. Fetch one and bring it to me, and you shall succeed. Do you accept?"

There was some trick—there was always a trick—but Spark trusted her wits and reflexes to deal with whatever Feyland threw at her.

"Yes," she said.

The air chimed with the faint echo of bells, and the hairy man nodded.

"Well?" he said. "Don't just stand there."

He probably wouldn't like it if she laughed at him, but he sounded like a grumpy old aunt of hers. Hiding her smile, Spark turned and headed in the direction he'd indicated.

Over the curve of the hill she found an orchard. Apple trees spread, planted in orderly rows, though not all of them bore fruit. Some were spangled with white flowers, while others unfurled leaves the new green of spring. From her vantage point she scanned the trees, but all the fruit she could see hanging from the boughs was red. The tree with copper apples must be farther in.

As she stepped into the orchard, the raucous cry of crows sounded. Up ahead, a dozen black shapes took to the sky. A murder of crows. She shivered, and stayed under the shelter of the branches as much as possible. Fending off an aerial attack was never fun, especially as her character had no shielding abilities.

The birds swirled up into a dark funnel, and Spark headed directly for it. The trees around her weren't anything special, despite the various seasons they represented. No—she'd find her copper apples in the part of the orchard where things were happening. Which meant heading for the crows.

Bees hummed among the flowers, and a few petals drifted like snow. The place was peaceful, until rough caws punctured the air. The light dimmed as a thick cloud shaded the sun. Ahead, she glimpsed a dark, gnarled shape: a tree with twisted branches rising into the sky. The area surrounding the tree was blighted, the green grass withered to gray. Her heart gave a thump. At the tip of the highest branch an apple hung, bright as a new penny.

The crows swirled around it, guarding their treasure. This close, Spark could see that their claws and beaks were sheathed in metal.

Great. Combat crows.

She paused beneath a flowering tree and studied her target. The branch bearing the apple was way too thin to take her weight, plus the crows wouldn't let her get near the tree without dealing some painful injuries.

Injuries that would carry over into the real world, according to Jennet. Spark wasn't in a hurry to find out the truth of her friend's words. So, a direct assault on the tree was out.

Slowly, she drew her bow and nocked an arrow. First thing was to get that shiny apple down to where she could grab it. Then she'd have to improvise.

Spark sighted down the arrow and took a deep, steadying breath. The circle of copper glimmered in her vision until her entire being focused on that one spot.

She exhaled and loosed her arrow.

CHAPTER THIRTEEN

SPARK'S ARROW FLEW TRUE, hitting the apple with a hollow clang. The fruit wobbled, but didn't fall. *Dammit!*

Screeching, the crows flurried into the air. They'd be on her in moments. She pushed down the fear starting to ripple through her and nocked another arrow, aiming for the stem this time. It was a tricky target—but she only had time for one last shot.

The arrow left the string with a hum, and Spark dashed after it. The crows increased their racket and began diving at her. She ducked low, feeling claws tangle in her hair. Ahead, the copper apple fell, the stem neatly severed.

With a final burst of speed, Spark flung herself forward and caught the fruit in one hand. Using her bow, she beat back the dark birds and hurried to summon up one of her elemental spells. Air—that would do it. Clutching the apple to her chest, she chanted the awkward syllables.

A gust of wind swept through the clearing, whipping her

hair into her face, and pushing the crows back. Spark turned and ran, the angry calls of the birds following her.

She made it about halfway through the orchard when the blossom-scattered grass before her erupted into a tangle of thorns. Leaping back, she saw that the wicked briars had sprouted all around her, and were closing in quickly. One long, sharp thorn pricked her wrist, painful as a needle.

"*Kijherba Oncoti!*" she cried.

Instantly, a wall of flame sprang up before her. Spark gestured it forward, and heard the briars screeching as the fire scorched them. They shriveled, and she leaped over the blackened tangle and kept running.

Spark's breath rasped in her throat as she raced for the edge of the orchard. She leaned forward, forcing another burst of speed. Behind her, the crows still called. A quick look over her shoulder showed a mass of thorns following in her wake, twisting and writhing along the ground.

She burst out of the orchard, only to rock back at the sight of a huge silver serpent blocking her way. Seriously—the game wasn't making it easy for her.

The serpent hissed, showing a long, forked tongue, then reared back, preparing to strike. Spark scrolled rapidly through her spells. She'd already burned the charms for air and fire, which left earth and water.

A thorn grazed her boot, and the crows called harshly behind her. Pulling on all her reserves, she wove the words of her remaining elements together, and flung them toward the serpent. Instantly it began to sink, surrounded by a pit of mud. It flailed back and forth, splashing clods of grass and thick gobs of mud up in huge gouts, but it was stuck, and sliding lower by the second.

Tucking the copper apple into her pocket, Spark sprinted to her right, cutting a wide path around the serpent now mired in muck. As she ran, she morphed into her fox form. Four paws dug into the grass, and her keen ears heard the swish of feathers behind her. She zigzagged, foiling the attacking crow. It screeched in anger. Another sound, a weird grinding, vibrated beneath her feet. Ahead, thorny briars burst out of the ground.

She leaped, just clearing the tangle. To her left, the serpent lunged, missing her by inches. It smelled like dry bones.

Her tiny heart pounding, she reached the crest of the hill. As soon as she topped it, the stench of the hairy man hit her like a wall of compost, making her eyes water. The sounds of pursuit faded, but she kept running until she reached the cottage.

"Heehee," the hairy man said. "A frightened fox. Has it forgotten how to be mortal?"

She almost had forgotten once, during the battle with the Dark Queen, but that time she'd stayed in her fox form far longer.

"Not even," she said as she transformed back into her human body. "I have the apple."

He scowled and held out his hand. Spark retrieved the fruit and gave it to him.

"You have succeeded." He didn't sound happy about it. "Take the apple."

She hesitated. Was this some kind of fey trick?

"Go on." He thrust his hand toward her. The copper apple shone brightly against his coarsely haired palm.

"Why?"

"Your quest was to fetch the apple and show it to me. The reward remains yours. Take it quickly, 'ere I transport you to the next level."

Spark snatched the gleaming fruit from him. During the final battle with the Dark Queen, both Tam and Jennet had used talismans they'd won in-game. Maybe the apple would prove equally helpful.

Of course, Jennet also had a magic sword she'd gotten from the Elder Fey. Somehow, Spark didn't think she was in line for a gift like that.

The hairy man lifted his hands, inscribing symbols into the air that left a glowing afterimage. The cottage tipped, the sky reversing, and she was enfolded in dizzying light once again. She gripped the apple, concentrating on its smooth solidity.

After three whirling heartbeats, she landed on solid ground. Swallowing hard, Spark looked around. She was in another clearing, this one in a piney forest. The moon-pale mushrooms surrounded her, and the sky overhead was the dark blue of early evening. A handful of scattered stars dusted the sky.

Good. She was progressing through the world, every level taking her closer to the Dark Court.

Spark tucked the copper apple away. With a deep breath, she stepped over the faerie ring and started down the dusky, beckoning path.

Aran followed Thomas back to the tent, his thoughts spinning. He didn't like being forced to reverse-hack into the real world. On the other hand, think of the cheats and exploits he'd learn, which he could sell once he got back.

Provided they worked in the non-magical portion of the game. Even if they didn't, he'd get a reward from the queen that would set him up in style.

Once inside the fabric walls of Thomas's home, Aran headed for his room. He wanted to see if he could get his tablet to turn on, and start making notes about how to do the impossible.

"Not so quickly," Thomas said, grabbing his arm as he went past.

"What?"

"BlackWing. I thought the name was familiar. How long have you been hacking games, young man?"

"Um." Aran pulled out of Thomas's grasp. It was too late to lie, not that he even wanted to. Something about the bard inspired the uncomfortable truth.

"Sit down." Thomas went to one of the nearby low chairs draped in colorful fabric, and gestured for Aran to join him.

"Three years," Aran said, warily taking a seat. He'd started learning how in juvie, and turned out to be surprisingly good at it. "How do you know about stuff like that? Games and hackers?"

"How do you think I came here?" Thomas said, a wry twist to his mouth. "The old ways of passage into the Realm of Faerie are gone—the standing stones toppled, the faerie rings and groves razed. The fey folk must find another way to access the mortal world."

"But a computer game?" Aran shook his head. "That's tweaked."

Thomas sighed and leaned back. "What is a game but a doorway into another, temporary, reality? With the FullD system, human technology reached an almost magical place. A *between* place, where things are and are not at the same time. That is the province of the fey."

"So somehow the faerie magic connected with Feyland?"

"If the game had not been based on ancient lore, perhaps it would not have." An old pain shone in Thomas's eyes.

"Wait." Aran sat up straight, suspicion scraping the back of his neck. "What's your full name?"

"Thomas Rimer."

"Damn." Aran jumped to his feet. "I don't believe it."

But he did, and things started to make all kinds of sense.

Thomas watched him with a weary gaze as Aran paced the leaf-green rug. Thomas—who was Thomas Rimer, the former lead developer for Feyland. Until he died.

"Am I dead?" Aran asked. "Is this some crazy version of the afterlife?"

"No. You are a living, breathing creature, here within the realm."

"Are you?"

"My physical body is gone," Thomas said. "My life essence, or spirit as some might call it, is here, bound to the service of the Dark Queen."

Aran's throat went dry. "Did she kill you? Like some kind of vampire thing?"

"I made the choice freely," Thomas said. "Just as you made the choice to enter the Dark Realm."

"Yeah, well, maybe that wasn't such a good idea." Aran rubbed his arms, warding off the sudden chill.

"Too late. You must accept the consequences of your choices."

"I'm sick of having to deal with the consequences when I'm misled about what I'm stepping into." Bitterness rose in the back of his throat.

He'd been naïve, and way too trusting of his older brother, when Setch had asked him to hand-deliver a package. Sure, he knew his brother was up to his neck in something shady, but he hadn't thought it would affect him.

Until he landed in jail, confused and too innocent, and conveniently underage enough to avoid the biggest penalties for transporting narcotics.

Seemed like the Realm of Faerie was similar to juvie, in terms of having its own, dangerous rules that he had to figure out—and fast.

Thomas raised an eyebrow. "Creatures who do not belong in your world appear through a glowing sphere, asking you to come with them. What, pray tell, is misleading about the fact that you ended up in a magical otherworld?"

"Fine." Aran crossed his arms. Maybe this one was a little more his fault. "So how do I start hacking—"

"Hold." Thomas rose smoothly to his feet and turned to face the door flap. "Someone approaches."

Aran stepped back, glancing around for something he could use as a weapon. He saw nothing useful, just a lot of musical instruments. If things got bad, he supposed he could smash a guitar over his attacker's head.

The door twitched open and a small figure bounded into

the room. His hair was a wild tangle festooned with feathers and he wore a costume of leaves and tatters. Bright, merry eyes shone in a sharp-featured face.

"Greetings!" he cried. "I see you have collected another mortal, Bard Thomas."

"Well met, Puck," Thomas said, his voice warm. He gestured to Aran. "This is my guest, BlackWing."

"Is he?" Puck asked.

He leaped into the air and kept going, as though ascending a solid, invisible staircase. He halted inches from Aran's nose and, hands on his hips, scrutinized Aran.

"Hey," Aran said, standing his ground. "You're in my space, little guy."

"Little I may be, but I am no guy. I am a sprite. And you, mortal, are in our space far more fully at present than we may venture into yours."

"That's not what I meant." Aran thought he knew what Puck was saying, despite his weird, roundabout faerie-speak. "And your goblin pals didn't seem to have a problem traipsing into my world."

Thomas winced. "There was more sacrifice involved in opening that portal than you might guess."

"Aye." Puck reached one long-fingered hand and grabbed a handful of Aran's hair, then gave it a quick, painful tug.

"Ow!"

Aran swiped at the creature, but Puck, grinning widely, had already somersaulted back down his invisible staircase.

"I know not why she should risk so much, for your sake," the sprite said.

"Who? The queen?"

Puck gave an impatient snort, then turned to Thomas. "One of the Feyguard comes. Summoned, no doubt, for this mortal."

"Aid her as you may." Thomas shot Aran an unreadable look. "I've no doubt she will be successful in her task."

"I shall assist, be assured of it." Puck cocked his head. "I do not think I can bring her to the queen's doorstep undetected. Meet us in the hour before midnight, in the borderlands nearest the realm."

"What are you guys even talking about?" Aran asked. "And what does it have to do with me?"

"Everything," Puck said. "And now, I must away."

He waved his hand and glittering dust swirled around him. When the air cleared, the sprite was gone.

"Where'd he go?" Aran asked, facing Thomas. "And what's going on?"

Thomas walked past him to the table, where the ever-present teapot was always hot and the plate of cakes never emptied.

"You will know, soon enough," the bard said. "Tea?"

Aran was tired of conversations that didn't go anywhere, of secrets and half truths. And he still couldn't entirely accept that he was hanging out in a magical land with a dead programmer.

"What happened to the other human?" he asked. "The kid who was here."

"Ah." Thomas set down the teapot, his cup only half full. "He has returned home."

Relief rippled through Aran. "So, he's not dead? Glad to hear the faeries don't go in for human sacrifice."

"Oh, they do." Thomas's tone was grim.

Aran swallowed, hard. He'd had enough answers for now.

"Right. I'm going to bed."

"Rest well, BlackWing."

As if he could. Aran pushed open the curtain to his room, glad for some privacy. He sat on the bed and picked up the plastic dragon figurine from the table, where he'd left it beside his tablet.

He turned the knobby plastic between his fingers, then ran his thumb over the seam along the figurine's back. It felt good to have that connection to the mortal world. A plastic dragon and his tablet. Sad, really.

Knowing it wouldn't work, he reached over and pressed the tablet's power button. Nothing. With a sigh, Aran put the dragon back on the table. It teetered for a moment, then fell over onto the blank screen.

Light flickered across the tablet face, and Aran blinked. He picked the dragon up, and the tablet went dark again. Slowly, he set the plastic figure on the screen and the surface immediately brightened. The tablet powered on—but only when the plastic dragon touched it.

Freaky. But then, this whole place was beyond strange.

Aran pinned the dragon against the screen with his thumb and moved the tablet onto his lap. Could he actually connect back to the real world?

He opened his messager to find a blinking note from Bix.

:That was a lame-ass goodbye. You better send postcards. And message me now and then. Gotta live vicariously through your adventures.:

For a stabbing second, Aran regretted his decision to go

with the goblins. He wished he really could send Bix a post-card from some nice, normal tourist destination.

There were no postcard racks in the Dark Court. If, in some freaky alternate universe, there were, he could just imagine what they'd look like. A close-up of the trapped fairies screaming, their tiny hands pressed against the lantern glass. The eerie figure of the horned hunter silhouetted against the unearthly stars. A candid shot of the Dark Queen reclining on her throne, with "wish you were here" emblazoned across the front.

So wrong, though amusing in a sick way. Even though postcards were out, maybe he could send a message.

:Sorry to leave so abruptly. Having quite the time, here. Catch you later.:

He had no idea if the message would get through, but he liked to imagine it would.

The net connection worked, too. Aran scrolled through the entertainment news until he got to a piece about Spark's tour. Actually, it covered the whole FullD launch, but he skimmed the boring stuff.

There was a picture of Spark, unhappily sandwiched between those other two gamers, the Terabins. Some kind of rivalry going on there. She hadn't looked very happy when she left the lunch panel stage at SimCon—though seeing him seemed to brighten her up.

As if. Spark Jaxley hadn't given him another moment's thought after she'd left. He'd been a diversion to her. One that hadn't ended up being all that pleasant, once her goons got hold of his records. Their connection was over before it had even begun.

Aran tapped his fingers over the screen. Enough with the past; he had to sort out the future. How to open the gate, escape the queen, and leave the realm with a nice profit in his pocket.

What if opening the gate wasn't such a good idea? Worry pinged the back of his brain, and he stuffed it back down. Thomas hadn't gotten too tweaked over the idea, so it couldn't be that bad—especially if the Realm of Faerie would die without that connection. Sure, the place was creepy, but it was magic, too. It didn't deserve to be destroyed.

And after all, didn't the human world need a little more enchantment?

CHAPTER FOURTEEN

SPARK strode through the dim forest, the scent of cedar and loam filling her nose. In the half light every branch resembled a reaching arm, every bush a crouching creature ready to spring.

Unlike the first game level, this one didn't open out into a meadow. Instead, she glimpsed a small clearing ahead. As she got closer, a dilapidated hut at the edge of the trees came into view; just the type of place one would find a wicked crone lying in wait to eat passing children.

The windows were dark, and cobwebs hung from the corners of the eaves, but a thin line of smoke trailed from the crooked chimney. Somebody was home.

"Hello?" Spark called, stepping into the clearing. "Anybody there?"

A night bird screeched nearby, making her jump, but there was no other reply. Still, she hadn't just stumbled onto this place by accident. Feyland had its own weird logic, and she'd do best to follow it.

ANTHEA SHARP

Holding her breath, as if that would make her presence quieter, she stepped onto the sagging porch. The boards creaked loudly under her feet.

The weathered door had a metal knocker in the center, depicting the head of a woman with long, flowing hair. The brass was cold under her fingers as Spark lifted the knocker, then let it fall with a thud that echoed through the hut.

Should she knock again? She started to lower her hand, and the knocker's hair came to life, slithering around her wrist and binding her fast.

"Hey! Let go," Spark cried as her hand was pulled back toward the woman's face.

The metal eyes opened, blank and pupil-less, and the knocker smiled. Its teeth looked very sharp.

"There is a price for admittance," it said, in a high, whispery voice.

Spark tugged at her hand, but the strands of metal held tight. Great. She was the captive of a freaky doorknocker.

"What kind of price?" she asked.

A sharp pain shot through her palm. With a yelp, Spark ripped her hand free. Blood trickled from a wound at the base of her thumb.

"You bit me." She couldn't quite believe it, despite the evidence. Despite the things Tam and Jennet had told her about how Feyland worked.

"Consider your admission paid." The knocker closed its eyes, its hair coming to rest again in still metal curves.

Slowly, quietly, the door swung open.

The hut was much bigger inside than it had appeared from the outside. A vast marble hallway stretched away from the door, lined with columns and the glow of ornate lamp sconces. In a niche at the far end of the hall something shone silver—something round, with a stem at the top.

A silver apple.

There was a theme here. Get the apple, gain the next level of Feyland. Somehow, Spark didn't think it would be as easy as sauntering down the hall and grabbing the fruit.

She set one booted foot on the marble floor, then quickly drew it back. Sharp blades flashed up from the floor, rising and falling in an unsynchronized rhythm. Each sword was three feet long, and wickedly honed. The air filled with the sound of steel snicking against steel. Sure enough, she'd activated the first defense system.

Spark watched and counted, but couldn't see an obvious pattern. If she stepped out there without a plan, she'd be sliced like lunchmeat. The only upside was that the floor of blades ended halfway down the hall. No doubt other traps awaited. She'd deal with those when she got to them.

Okay, how did she solve this predicament? Trying to ignore the metallic clashing, she looked through her inventory. Bow and arrows, boot dagger, cloak. Not helpful. Copper apple. Maybe?

She selected it from her inventory, and the apple appeared in her hand. Holding it up, she inspected it closely, something she hadn't had a chance to do while evading the crows and briars earlier.

A seam ran horizontally around the apple, as if it could split in half. What did it hold, and how could she get it open? She tried sticking her thumbnail in the hairline crack, and then the blade of her dagger, but the fruit remained stubbornly closed.

Maybe it was like a genie in a bottle. Which meant she had three wishes, right? Spark glanced at the flashing swords. It wouldn't be enough just to wish them gone, since something even worse would appear in their place. Magical games were tricky that way.

No, she had to think of a solution for crossing over that expanse of slicing swords. Over...

Spark rubbed the rounded top of the apple with her thumb.

"A DeFacto 442-Z grav-board, please," she said.

The apple trembled in her hand and—just as she'd guessed—split neatly in half. Glittering dust swirled out, accompanied by a flash of light. The apple snapped closed again before she could glimpse its inner workings.

Spark blinked, half blinded by the brightness. When her vision cleared she let out a small whoop of triumph.

There, on the weathered boards of the porch, sat the world's most high-end grav-board. The shiny plas-metal and neon lettering looked glaringly out of place against the simple hut and wooded clearing. Out of place—and incredibly welcome.

"Thanks," she said, giving the apple a kiss before tucking it back into her inventory.

Now for the hard part. She grabbed the board and strode back into the clearing, giving herself a good fifteen feet of lead-in to the doorway.

She hoped the board worked, here in the magic-laden world of Feyland.

Scratch that—belief was a powerful force. She *knew* the board would work. Refusing doubt, she flicked the grav switch. With a hum, the board rose six inches into the air.

Oh, yeah. She was about to take the ride of her life. Good thing she'd played a ton of games that utilized grav-board mechanics, as well as her real-world boarding experience. Surfing over and through a sea of swords was just another skill challenge.

Pushing away the knowledge that failure could be deadly, Spark hopped onto the board. She took a second to find her balance, then leaned forward, pointing the board at the illuminated doorway of the hut. The board kicked up speed—damn, it was even more powerful in-game than the actual model she owned—and the clearing blurred around her.

Speed, height, and maneuverability were the factors she had to juggle. She managed to cross over the first couple blades with inches to spare, but the next sword rose higher than she'd expected. She wasn't going to make it.

Breath catching in her throat, she dropped into a crouch and heard the sing of metal as the blade swung just over her head. A strand of magenta hair fluttered down, quickly turned to pink dust by the razor-sharp swords. Spark gulped back her fear, trying not to imagine what would happen if she fell.

She banked hard to the right, aiming for an empty spot by one of the columns, and misjudged. The whole board shuddered as a blade hit it with a bone-jarring clang.

"Come on," she said, under her breath. "Halfway across. You can do it."

She didn't know if she was talking to the grav-board or to herself.

The blades began to move faster, carving through the air in a series of deadly arcs. She only had a moment to catch her breath beside the column. Every sense alert, she pointed the board back into the center of that lethal flurry.

Dodge. Lean. Crest and plummet. One blade left a neat slice in her sleeve, just missing her skin. She tasted blood, but it was because she was biting the inside of her cheek in concentration. Instinct guided her, and a knowledge of attack patterns gleaned over playing thousands of games. Pause. Now race forward.

A sword loomed before her. No time to avoid it. Spark shifted back on the board, wincing as the blade cut down hard into the plas-metal deck. The lifters shrieked a protest as the board dipped unsteadily.

She kicked the sword away, then, sensing motion in her peripheral vision, flung herself flat on the board's rough surface. Two blades cut the air overhead, meeting with a crash that made the whole room vibrate. In the second of quiet that followed, Spark nudged the board over the last set of blades. It settled safely on the marble floor with a quiet whine and the smell of scorched electronics.

Slowly, she climbed to her feet. Her legs trembled and cold sweat dampened her face. That had been the most harrowing ride ever.

"Thanks," she said, picking up the grav-board.

She couldn't tell if it was damaged beyond repair, but, regardless, she wasn't going to leave it behind. There was plenty of room in her inventory. Giving the blade-nicked edge a last pat, she stowed the board away.

The swords still rose and fell between her and the doorway, though with much less vigor than before. That danger was behind her.

Now she only had to face whatever was ahead.

Spark scanned the marble hall. The silver apple shone temptingly from its niche, but she knew better than to just dash forward and try to grab it. Instead, she pulled her bow from her back and extended it in front of her.

With a whoosh, a thick wall of glass slid across the hall, nearly severing the tip of her bow—and blocking her from reaching the apple. She yanked her bow back, then, when nothing else happened, used the end to tap on the glass. The weapon didn't burst into flames or start dissolving, so she stepped up and touched her fingers to the glass.

It was cool and smooth, and her fingertips left smudges on the surface. Spark strode the length of the wall and felt along the seam where the glass met marble. No gap. The other side was the same.

She leaned back, looking up the flat expanse. The ceiling was gone, which shouldn't have surprised her. The glass wall extended up and up, into a pale sky filled with puffy clouds. It was impossible to tell if the wall ever ended.

There had to be some way to get through. She tried her dagger blade, but it didn't scratch the surface. Banging the pommel against the glass didn't do anything, either. Her close-range arrow bounced off, careening dangerously past Spark's head before disappearing into the field of swords. And the wall seemed to absorb every spell she threw at it.

Well. Hoping she was right about the three wishes, she rubbed the copper apple again. For a second she considered asking for magic beans, but there was an easier way than climbing a vine and fighting a giant up in the clouds. Besides, that storyline had already been done.

"Laser cutter," she said.

The apple opened, emitted its glitter and light, then snapped shut. At Spark's feet lay a laser cutter, just like the kind her dad used in his contracting business. She put the apple back in her inventory, then picked up the laser.

It hummed when she turned it on, and it didn't take long for her to cut a ragged oval in the glass wall. Mental fingers crossed, she set her palm in the center and pushed. For a second the glass resisted, and then the oval fell out. It hit the marble floor and shattered, crashing into long, glittering splinters. Clearly the fey folk hadn't heard about safety glass.

Spark put the cutter away and ducked through the hole she'd made, careful to avoid treading on the shards of broken glass. She drew her boot dagger and took a cautious step down the hall, the words of her spells at the tip of her tongue, her senses alert.

One hard challenge, one easy one. These things usually went in threes, and she hoped the last challenge wouldn't prove deadly.

With her next step, she heard music—a lilting melody backed by a swift-strumming rhythm. She glimpsed motion out of the corner of her eye, and whirled around. Nothing.

She turned back to face the end of the hall, and caught her breath at the light and energy before her. Graceful dancers turned and dipped on the floor, their faces strange and beautiful, their hair sheened with starlight. Most had wings sprouting from the backs of their elegant evening clothes: jewel-bright butterfly wings, gossamer wisps of light, the translucent panes of a dragonfly, and the dusty feathers of night moths.

Glowing orbs flickered and bobbed over the dancers, and the music was so strong it set her feet to tapping. She bent and tucked her knife back into its boot sheath. Beyond the throng of dancers, the silver apple shone.

Timing her steps to the music, Spark slipped between the nearest couple. Whenever she saw an opening, she darted through. *Yes!* She was getting closer and closer.

At last she gained the edge of the marble dance floor. She looked up in triumph—only to see that somehow she'd ended up back where she had begun. Instead of standing in front of the niche holding the silver apple, she faced the hole in the glass wall, the floor around her still sparkling and dangerous.

Dammit. She turned to face the dancers once more. Tapping her lip with one finger, she watched the swirls and patterns of the dance. Maybe she'd gotten turned around in there. One more try, and if that didn't work, she'd have to change tactics.

This time, the dancers appeared to be more aware of her. She was jostled a number of times, and once a cat-eyed maiden hissed at her. When Spark reached the edge, she wasn't too surprised to find herself before the glass wall once more.

Okay then.

If she couldn't get through on her own, she'd have to find a partner and dance her way across. She tried stepping onto the floor and waving, but it seemed she was once again invisible to the dancers.

The gorgeously gowned and extravagantly suited dancers.

She glanced down at her clothing: the leggings tucked into rugged boots, the rustic vest and woolen cloak. Definitely not the thing to wear to a ball.

Taking a deep breath, she summoned the copper apple again. If she was wrong, she'd waste the final wish. Giving the fruit a rub, she whispered the words.

"I need a fancy ball gown."

The apple did its glittery thing, though instead of closing it simply vanished. Her last wish, gone. She desperately hoped it had been the right one.

With a whoosh, a gown made of gauze and satin floated down out of the air. Its bodice was deepest rose, the skirts shading out to purple. The overskirt was a silver material that flowed and glimmered like water. It was gorgeous, though not exactly the best outfit for doing battle.

If this worked, though, she wouldn't have to fight. Spark pulled off her cloak and placed it, and her bow and arrows, into her inventory. She tugged the gown over her vest and breeches, and kept her boots on, her dagger firmly tucked in place.

The gown settled about her like rays of sunset, the skirts just skimming the floor. Now all she needed was a partner.

As if the thought had summoned him, a tall faerie approached. He was clad in silken fabric that flowed from deep purple to midnight black. His long, pale hair hung unbound down his back, held away from his face by a circlet of braided ivy.

He was completely dreamy—if you counted nightmares in that description. His eyes were full of terrors, and Spark swallowed, hard, when he held out his hand.

"Dance, milady?" he asked, in a voice that sounded soft. The way a cat's paw was soft, until it shot out its wickedly sharp claws.

But she didn't have much choice if she wanted to get to the far end of the hall and snatch the silver apple.

She put her hand in his, trying not to flinch when his extra-long fingers closed over hers. His skin was cold and pale, as though he were crafted of the marble surrounding them. With a sharp smile, he drew her into the dance, one hand at the small of her back.

Spark gingerly set her hand on his shoulder. It hadn't escaped her notice that his teeth ended in sharp points. The music rose about them, moving into a waltz tempo. Good— she kind of knew how to waltz, as opposed to the fancier moves she'd seen the dancers making earlier.

Despite her inexperience—did waltzing with her pillow when she was in middle school count?—she found herself gliding with ease. Her partner guided her surely about the floor, and there was probably some faerie magic in the air that helped. The hardest part was keeping track of where she was in relation to the apple.

Every time she got the location fixed, her partner would swirl her around and she'd lose sight of the silver apple again. His grip was firm and implacable, though he didn't look at her as they waltzed. She was just as glad not to be the focus of those incredibly scary eyes.

Spark counted under her breath. Every twenty-four steps they'd circle back to the niche holding the apple. She counted twice more, to be sure.

The next pass around the hall, she was ready. At twenty-one, she braced herself. Twenty-two, lifted her arm. Twenty-three, ducked out into a twirl. Twenty-four, reached, ignoring the painful pull of the faerie's grip.

She leaned out, stretching toward the shining silver fruit. Her fingertips brushed it, and it wobbled.

No—she'd missed.

In slow motion, the apple teetered and plummeted from its niche. The music slowed, and the dancers let out gasps of horror. Spark lunged, ripping free of her partner's grasp, and hit the floor hard, one hand outstretched. Her other wrist bent too sharply, trapped between her and the marble, and she felt something give way with a snapping pain.

The apple fell into her palm, heavy and solid. Despite the agony in her left wrist, Spark smiled. Quest complete.

She looked up, expecting the fey dancers to rush her, demanding their prize back. But the hall was empty. She'd beaten all three challenges and won the silver apple.

With a whimper, she sat up. She tried to wiggle the fingers of her left hand, and hot fire flashed along her nerves, making her gasp.

Great. She'd won this round—but now she had a damaged wrist, and she hadn't finished questing through to the Dark Court. Spark tucked the apple away, then rose to her feet, bracing herself against the smooth marble wall.

Now what? The idea of facing the queen one-handed wasn't appealing. And if Jennet and Tam were right, her wrist would be injured in the real world, too. She had to log off and get medical attention. And somehow explain how she'd ended up getting hurt.

Before she could take a step forward, the air around her

whirled with golden light. Everything lurched, the walls bowing inward, then out. Spark squeezed her eyes closed, fighting the sudden nausea. Now was not the best time for the game to decide to transport her to the next level. Though she could log out there, and hopefully return to the same place when she got another chance to play.

But when would that be? Vonda wouldn't let her sneak another session on the FullD, and then there was the little problem of her wrist. Spark doubted VirtuMax would allow her to sim until it healed—which would thrill the Terabins. No, she had to finish this now.

Biting her lip hard to distract herself from the pain, Spark opened her eyes.

CHAPTER FIFTEEN

"Thomas," Aran said, ducking out of his room.

The bard looked up from the low couch and left off strumming his guitar.

"What is it?"

"I need to see the place where the game interfaces with the Realm of Faerie," Aran said. "If you know where that is."

Time for him to get started on his assignment for the queen—and figure out if he could actually succeed.

Thomas plucked out a melancholy chord, then set his guitar aside and rose.

"Very well. I am honor-bound to aid you, though I like it not. Although I doubt you will be able to accomplish this task you've accepted so foolishly."

Aran gave him a close look. "Since you're the one responsible for hooking the game up to the realm in the first place, why doesn't the queen get you to do this reverse-hacking?"

"My connection with the mortal world is broken. Even had I wanted to, I could not do this thing for her."

"Fair enough. Don't sound so excited about it, though." Aran let the edge of sarcasm in his voice mask his anxiety. He still had zero idea how he was going to pull this off.

"Come," Thomas said, holding the tent flap open. "Though I urge you to consider returning to the mortal world. You will see soon enough how impossible the queen's request is."

Aran followed him out into the constant night. "Maybe."

Was the bard only helping because he was certain Aran would fail? Well, he'd prove Thomas wrong. Somehow.

They walked silently through the dark oak forest surrounding the court. When they ran out of trapped-faerie lights, Thomas raised his hand and conjured a ball of silvery-blue radiance. It reflected eerily off the branches and points of light in the bushes that looked like watching eyes.

"I don't suppose you have any advice for me?" Aran asked. "You know, being the lead programmer and everything."

"No."

Thomas did not elaborate, and Aran supposed he was lucky the bard was even helping him at all.

Soon, the oaks were replaced by pale-barked trees with shimmering leaves. Everything was washed of color, the trees and leaves rendered in black and gray. Moonlight slanted down into a clearing ahead. At the edge of the trees, Thomas halted.

"Step into the faerie ring," he said, pointing to the circle of mushrooms at the center of the glade. "When you reach your destination, mark well the location of the clearing, so that you may come back to this place."

"Wait—you're not coming?" A splinter of panic lodged in Aran's throat.

"This is your quest, BlackWing, not mine. I shall await your return."

A million scared questions clamored in Aran's mind, but he refused to ask any of them. Thomas had made it clear he was on his own, and totally expected Aran to tweak it. Swallowing back his fear, he strode past the bard and into the moonlit clearing.

When he stepped into the center of the mushroom-bounded circle, a cold wind pricked his skin. The air wavered, and the wind increased, buffeting him furiously. Aran hunched his shoulders against the gusts. After a few moments the air quieted. Shaking his hair out of his face, he looked up and saw that he still stood in the center of the faerie ring. But everything else had changed.

Twilight deepened the air, the last light of sunset tipping over the horizon, and the world held more color. The moss under his feet was a deep, velvety green. The mushrooms surrounding him shone like small moons, and the pale-barked trees did, in fact, have silvery leaves.

In front of him, like a mirror image, stood another clearing. Unlike his, the late afternoon sun illuminated the rich colors of flowers surrounding the faerie ring. And the mushrooms were different, a mix of the pale ones surrounding him and bright red ones, speckled with white.

Even weirder, another clearing lay beyond that one. Sunlight streamed brightly down, making Aran squint. All the mushrooms in that ring were the red ones with white spots.

Okay. He folded his arms, unwilling to step out of his own clearing until he'd figured things out.

He thought back to when Spark had played the demo

game. The opening sequence... what had the clearing looked like? He was pretty sure the original game of Feyland had a faerie ring with both kinds of mushrooms, just like the middle clearing.

The ring surrounding him was made entirely of the moon-pale ones, and it had brought him to this place from the Dark Court. If he had to guess, he'd say the mushrooms were sign-posts, of a sort.

So where did the red and white ones lead? Was there yet another world tucked away behind the game's interface?

"The Bright Court," a high voice said.

Aran spun, his heartbeat revving. "What? Who's there?"

"Puck, at your service."

The sprite nimbly bounded down one of the pale branches. The branch bent under his slight weight, bringing him face to face with Aran.

"The bright what?" Aran asked, trying to get his racing pulse back under control.

"Court." Puck gestured to the sunlit glade. "Yon gateway leads there."

That made sense, in a tweaked, faerie-world kind of way. If it was always night in the Dark Court, then it must always be day somewhere else.

"Who's in charge of that court?" Aran asked. "And why didn't I end up there?"

"The Bright King rules the Bright Court. He is not as cunning as his sister, nor as schooled in the art of snares and trickery. Though, when he chooses to use it, he has power aplenty."

Aran filed that information away to process another time.

It was good to get some solid answers to his questions. As long as Puck was forthcoming, he'd keep asking.

"So, the middle clearing. Is that the way back into the real world?"

The sprite gave him a faintly disgusted look. "Real? Everything you have experienced is true, and each of the courts is as real as your own realm."

"All right, sorry. It goes to the human world?"

"Indeed. Well puzzled, mortal." Puck leaned forward and tweaked Aran's nose, then catapulted back, laughing. The branch swayed as he deftly caught his balance.

"Hey!" Aran rubbed his nose. "Was that really necessary?"

The sprite ignored his question. "The center clearing is bounded by a wall, naught but a thin crack between it and the realm. Can you see the protections with your mortal eye?"

"No."

Aran stepped out of the circle of pale mushrooms and walked slowly toward the middle clearing, hands extended. Sure enough, where the clearings touched he encountered an invisible barrier. It was slightly rough, as though made of unpolished granite. He ran his palms over the surface, searching for the crack.

At last he found it, barely wide enough for the edge of his thumbnail.

"This is the crack that lets humans into the realm?" he asked. "I'm not sure how anyone could even fit through there."

"'Tis a metaphor," Puck said, in a tone that implied Aran was denser than rock.

"Why doesn't the queen send a bunch of goblins with pry bars over here and just, you know, force it open."

"It would not succeed. Let me show you."

Puck leaped from the branch, turned a somersault, and came to hover next to Aran. He lifted his hands, and greenish light spread from his long fingertips. When the light touched the wall, Aran sucked in his breath.

Lines of code encircled the center clearing. X-y scripts and commands glowed, as clearly as if they were displayed on a screen. Numbers and words and complex figures spun out, Puck's magic spreading like a virus until the entire wall was illuminated. And it was constructed of nothing but programming.

Freaky.

Aran set his fingertip to one of the lines and flicked. The code obediently moved up, and another line took its place.

"This is it," he breathed. "I just need a way to input."

And he had one. He whirled to face Puck.

"Can you get me to the tent, then back here?" Aran asked. "Quickly would be good."

The sprite looked at him, a mischievous glint in his dark eyes. "I can. Step with me into the ring, and I will take you where you need to go."

Aran leaped back into the center of the faerie ring. He could so do this. Grab his tablet—and the dinosaur—then run some of his hacker scripts into the wall. He was certain it would work.

And when it did... he'd be completely set. He'd return to the real world with enough wealth to at last take control of his life. No more subsisting on the edge, unable to get a job, or even a date, because of his criminal record.

Money meant freedom. Independence. The chance to

finally follow his dreams, instead of living on the edges of other people's hopes.

Exhilaration sang through his blood.

"Hurry it up." He beckoned to the sprite, who was sauntering over the soft mosses.

Puck gave him a saucy wink, then bounded into the faerie ring. The chill wind rose, tugging at Aran's hair and pushing at his shoulders. He huddled against it, waiting for it to end.

When it did, he blinked at their surroundings, then rounded on Puck.

"Where are we? I thought the plan was to get me back to the tent! This looks nothing like the clearing I came from."

Instead of the dark trees and endless night, the sky overhead shone pearly gray. The clearing they stood in was large, and on one side stood a falling-down hut.

"Wait," Puck said, holding up one long-fingered hand.

"No. Take me back, right—"

Aran broke off as a figure emerged from the building, one arm cradled close to her body. Her magenta hair was unmistakable.

"Spark?" he whispered.

What the hell was Spark doing here, in the fantastical areas of Feyland?

"She is injured," Puck said, springing forward.

Aran didn't hesitate. He sprinted past Puck and met Spark in front of the hut. She stood there, holding on to one of the crooked posts supporting the porch, and stared at him.

"Oh my God. Aran." Her face, which had been pale before, lost all color.

"Are you okay?" he asked, reaching for her arm.

She flinched back. "I think I broke my wrist—but that's not important. I came to rescue you. We have to get you out of here."

"Me? What about you?"

She shook her head, her bright hair swinging across the pointed features of her avatar.

"Puck," she said, turning to address the sprite. "I heard I might run into you. Thanks for the help."

"A pleasure, milady." Puck swept her an elaborate bow.

"How did you get here?" Aran asked her. "I thought humans couldn't enter the realm."

"I could ask you the same thing." She narrowed her eyes. "As soon as we get back to the mortal world, you and I are having a serious talk. Dammit—I *knew* something happened when you played the Feyland demo."

"You did?" Aran thought back. All her questions started to make sense. "Wait—is that why you kept inviting me to things? So you could pump me for information?"

He'd been an idiot. Spark wasn't interested in him romantically, she had just wanted to know what he'd seen in-game.

"That's not the only reason," she said.

"Yeah, right. How did you know I was in Feyland?"

"It's complicated. Once we're in our world I'll explain. Come on." She started across the clearing, toward the ring of mushrooms sprouting on the far side. "Puck, can you send us through?"

"I will do my best," he said. "Though my magic is small compared to the queen's, you hold the Elder Fey's favor. It will be enough to take you home."

"Whoa." Aran halted, lifting his hands. "I'm not going back."

"What?" Spark whirled on him, her expression fierce. "Of course you are. Do you have any idea how much danger you're in? I'm just glad I found you before you got to the Dark Court."

"Um." Aran shoved his hands in his pockets. "I've already been there."

"How did you escape?" Still holding her right arm against her chest, she grabbed him with her other hand. "Never mind. Let's just go."

As if to underscore her words, a long, mournful howl wavered through the air. Aran shivered at the sound.

"The hunt," Puck said. "Quickly, mortals, to the ring!"

Aran pulled out of Spark's grasp.

"Look—it's nice that you came to get me and all, but I'm staying here."

"You can't be serious."

"There's nothing back in our world for me," he said. "Nothing."

Her eyes widened, and she took a step closer to him. "If you were to see the Dark Queen, you'd understand how dangerous—"

"I've seen her. In fact, I'm working for her."

Spark stared at him, a look of disbelief on her face. The air curdled with another eerie howl, punctuated with the rumble of hoof beats.

"Now!" Puck cried, dancing about them furiously. "There is no more time to waste."

"You'd better go." Aran crossed his arms. "Get that wrist taken care of."

"I can't believe this." She took hold of his arm again, but he yanked free.

"I said no."

She glanced at the sky, then back to him, eyes flashing. "I'm coming back for you. Soon. You may be working for the queen, but *my* job is to return you to the mortal world. Whether you want to or not."

"I choose *not*."

A dark shadow swept over the clearing. Aran looked up to see a company of faerie folk mounted on black horses with fiery hooves riding across the sky. At their head rode the horned hunter, and before him dashed his flame-eyed hounds.

Spark let out a gasp and, clutching her arm against her body, sprinted for the faerie ring. As soon as she leaped into the center, Puck flung up his hands and chanted three syllables, high and chiming. Blue light flashed, and Spark was gone.

The sprite rounded on him. "Oh, foolish, foolish choice. She braved the realm for you—indeed, bears an injury because of it—and you turned her away."

Guilt twinged through him. Had Spark really gotten hurt because of him?

"It's not my fault she came in here." The words rang hollow.

"It is." Puck shook his head sadly. "Think well on that."

An instant later the sprite disappeared, just as the horned hunter landed in the clearing.

The hounds circled, growling at Aran. Despite the

panicked pumping of his heart, he didn't move. He was under the queen's protection. He clutched that thought as the master of the hunt rode toward him, antlered head silhouetted against the storm-tossed sky.

"Mortal," the hunter said, in a voice that held the echo of doom. "You have lost your way."

"Not really. More of a detour."

The hunter slowly turned his head to regard the faerie ring. When he looked back at Aran, his eyes were lightless pools.

"We shall escort you back to the court," he said, reaching out a hand gloved in thick leather.

Aran hesitated, and the hunter grabbed him, quick as a snake striking. An instant later, Aran was seated behind him on the huge black horse.

With a shrill whistle, the hunter pointed into the sky. The fey mount leaped, and Aran lurched forward, forced to take a handful of the hunter's cloak to steady himself. It was way closer than he ever wanted to be to any of the fey folk.

A rank, feral odor surrounded him as the hounds flowed around the horses' feet. From somewhere behind came the high keening of pipes. The wind ripped tears from the corners of his eyes. Aran glanced down to see the dark tops of the trees billowing beneath them like waves. Silver ponds blinked their still eyes as the hunt rode over, leaving shadows in their wake.

He held on, clenching his jaw as the Wild Hunt stormed across the sky like his worst nightmare made real.

CHAPTER SIXTEEN

SPARK FUMBLED, one-handed, at her gaming helmet, and managed to yank it off. Her wrist throbbed, and she knew she had to call Vonda and get it tended to right away. All she could do for the moment, though, was sit there, half in shock.

Aran was the mortal who had stumbled into the Dark Court. Aran! And not only that, he'd gone there on purpose.

Dammit—why hadn't she nailed him to the wall and demanded more information?

Well, and what if she had? He'd been evasive with his answers. Did she really think he would have told the truth?

Even if he'd confessed, it wasn't like she could have done anything, other than warn him.

Her wrist twinged. With a soft groan, she got out of the sim chair and stumbled to the hotel phone on the nightstand. It was beyond late, but she had to wake Vonda. Sinking onto the bed, she punched in her manager's room number.

"Hello?" Vonda's voice was groggy. "This better be an emergency."

"It's Spark. And yeah, you should probably call the med techs."

"The hell?" Vonda sounded suddenly wide awake. "I'll be right there."

Spark unlocked the door, then sat on the bed, waiting. She felt wretched, inside and out. Her first assignment as a Feyguard, and so far she was failing miserably. How could she rescue Aran if he refused to leave the realm? But how could she let him remain there, in such danger?

As soon as she got her wrist fixed up, she had to talk to Jennet and figure out what to do next.

Vonda burst into the room and hurried over to the bed.

"No blood," she said, after looking Spark over with a critical gaze. "What happened?"

"My wrist." Spark held it out, then winced when Vonda touched her.

"Aw, damn. Can you wiggle your fingers?"

She tried, and this time was able to manage a little motion, though the pain that followed made her gasp.

"I'm getting you some ice and aspirin, and pulling the FullD out of here. No way are you playing more tonight on an injury. The med techs should be here soon."

"Okay." Though things were so far from okay she wanted to scream.

When Vonda returned, Spark pressed the ice-filled towel against her wrist and tried to breathe normally. She watched, heart sinking even further, as the VirtuMax crew took the sim-system out. There went her last chance to get into Feyland.

She had to come up with another plan, and fast. The

longer Aran spent in the realm, the more danger he'd be in of being trapped there forever. Even if he didn't know it, she did.

Outside, she heard sirens approaching. They cut off, and a few minutes later she was surrounded by med techs taking her vitals and examining her wrist. They stuck her arm in a portable scanner, then clustered around the readout.

"It's a grade two sprain," one of them announced. "Not broken."

Spark let out her breath. The painkillers were starting to kick in, too, and she leaned back against the mounded pillows.

"What does that mean?" she asked. "I don't have to get a cast or anything, right? How soon until I can play again?"

"Gamers." Vonda shook her head.

"Young lady." The head tech, a guy with reddish hair, gave her a stern look. "You have to give yourself time to heal. Ice regularly, take anti-inflammatories, and wear a splint, especially when you sleep. With the right care, you'll be functioning normally again in a few weeks."

"A few weeks?" She turned to Vonda. "I can't sit around that long! I'm working, and we have a system to debut."

Vonda firmed her lips. "We'll deal with it, Spark. Now shut up and get some rest."

Despite the harsh words, Spark was reassured. Vonda would let her try playing—that was what "we'll deal with it" meant. Maybe she could fit her splinted hand into an over-sized glove. Or even play one-handed.

"Good advice," the med tech said. "We'll let your manager take care of the details of paperwork and prescriptions. If you'll step outside, ma'am?"

Vonda looked a little sour at being called ma'am. Before she followed the man out, she set her hand on Spark's forehead.

"Don't worry," she said. "We'll work this out."

Spark could only hope.

Aran stormed into the tent. He wished it had a real door, one he could slam. Or a hard floor to stomp over instead of the lush carpets. Anger was a bright flame, covering the guilt gnawing at him.

"And he yet remains in the realm? This is disastrous." Thomas broke off as Aran entered.

"You!" Aran pointed at Puck, who hovered cross-legged several feet in the air, drinking a cup of tea. "You tricked me, with your faerie-ring switcheroo. Taking me to Spark, when you were supposed to bring me back here."

"I only spoke true words," the sprite replied. "You parsed the meaning incorrectly. 'Twas no trickery, but a sidestep."

Aran scowled and turned to Thomas. Arguing with Puck was a useless activity.

"Do you know a girl named Spark?" he asked.

Thomas tilted his head and studied Aran for a long moment. Then he sighed and went to the table.

"Tea?" he asked.

"As long as you're serving up some answers, too."

"I will reveal what little I may. Understand, I walk a difficult path between my loyalty to the queen and the remnants of my mortal heart."

"Just tell me about Spark." Aran took an impatient swig of tea. There were lies upon lies here, and he was sick of being tangled in the middle.

"She is one of the Feyguard," Thomas said.

"No idea what that means." Though Aran could guess.

"The Feyguard are those few mortals set to watch the boundary between your world and the Realm of Faerie."

"So she knew about Feyland all along?"

"Aye," Puck said. "And you should have heeded her warnings."

Aran wrapped his fingers around his cup. Thinking back to SimCon, she *had* warned him—in a totally oblique way. Not that it would have made any difference, even if he'd understood what she was saying.

"Why are you still here?" Thomas asked. "Spark battled her way deep into the realm to free you, sustaining injuries along the way. Puck stood ready to open the gate. Every shred of mortal sense would have you gone from the realm, and yet you remain."

Damn right he'd stayed—mostly out of pride, and stubbornness, and the burning desire to fit somewhere. And the pure thrill of unlocking the puzzle of code. He was close on that one. Not to mention the reward.

Aran drained the last of his tea and set the cup on the table. "Even if it's dangerous here, at least I'm doing something. Helping the magic."

"The magic needs no assistance from you," Thomas said. "The queen has more than enough power at her command."

"Fine, then. Send me back." Aran folded his arms, betting on the fact the bard couldn't directly cross the queen. "I'll go."

Thomas gave him a long, weary look. "Would that I could, but your presence here is not so easily undone. Deep magic summoned you, and only deep magic can return you to the mortal world again. You missed one chance. Pray that you do not miss another."

CHAPTER SEVENTEEN

THE NEXT MORNING, Spark ordered room service. She felt clumsy, and didn't want to explain her injury. Or deal with the Terabins. As soon as her breakfast arrived, she pulled out her messager and keyed in Jennet.

:You there?: Spark sent.

A full minute later, the reply came.

:Barely. It's two hours earlier here, you know.:

:Yeah, sorry. But I have bad news.:

:No luck getting into Feyland?: Jennet's message appeared slowly. Clearly her fingers were slow to wake up, too.

:Oh, I got in-game no problem. I even found the person who was sucked into the Dark Realm.:

Spark paused, trying to think of how to phrase her next words. Ah, hell. Jennet was her friend. She deserved complete honesty.

:And?: Jennet prompted.

:And not only did it turn out to be the guy I met at SimCon, he's

still in the realm. I failed.: There, she'd gotten the worst of it over with.

:?! Give me a sec.:

Spark grabbed her tea and took a big gulp, then fiddled with the bunch of grapes on the room service tray.

:Did you lose a battle with the queen?: Jennet finally asked.

:No—I didn't fail that way. Aran simply refused to return to our world.:

:So push him into the faerie ring.:

:I was hurt.:

:What? Stop already with the epic reveals. Are you all right?: Jennet's messages were coming quicker now. Probably Spark's news was shaking the drowsiness right out of her head.

:It's just a sprained wrist. Hurt a lot, though.:

:Don't do it again.:

:Yeah, well, I don't know when I can get back in Feyland again. Could you and Tam—:

:Of course,: Jennet sent. *:Though neither of us have heard even a whisper from the Elder Fey. We'll see if we can find your guy and pull him out.:*

:He's not my guy.: Most definitely not, after their last encounter. *:Let me know. And thanks.:*

:Hey, friend, it's what we do. Right?:

:Right. See you when.:

Jennet sent a smiley wave icon in farewell.

Still tired, Spark leaned back against her pillows to finish her tea. She hoped Jennet and Tam could succeed where she'd failed. After all, they were the experts.

After picking at her breakfast, getting packed, then burning an hour watching stupid cat vids, it was time to go.

Spark was careful to stay behind the Terabins as they boarded the tour bus. With one hand out of commission, she knew she'd make a tempting target.

"Did you fall down?" Cora asked, looking at Spark's splint as she passed. "I know you're uncoordinated, but I thought you at least knew how to walk."

"She's taking the easy way out," Roc said, sprawling along a whole row. "Now she has an excuse for why our scores and gameplay will be so much better than hers."

Spark felt her cheeks heat with anger, but she didn't give them the satisfaction of a reply. Head high, she sidestepped Cora's attempt to trip her and headed for the middle of the bus. Niteesh was already there, and Spark settled across the aisle from him.

"Nice timing on that," he said, nodding to Spark's splinted wrist.

"Like I sprained it on purpose."

"No." He leaned forward and lowered his voice. "But this way the Terribles can rule supreme without having to take you out. And you can still appear onstage at Bella Boingo's concert tonight."

"Oh joy." The pop star's music had never been to Spark's taste. The singer's fan base overlapped with hers, though, so VirtuMax had set up the special guest appearance.

Originally, Spark was scheduled to run a quick demo on the FullD, but her injury made that impossible. Vonda had scrambled and arranged for footage of Spark's SimCon demo to be shown instead.

"I know why you sprained it." Niteesh flashed her a smile. "You won't have to sign autographs."

"I'm right-handed, goof." She rolled her eyes at him. "Still, it feels like a cheat, just to show up and do nothing at the concert."

"Nah. Your fans want to see you. That's enough."

"Well, that and the extra VirtuMax swag the company will be handing out." She yawned. The swaying of the tour bus, on top of her pain meds, was making her groggy.

"Here." Niteesh handed her a pillow. "I'll wake you up when we get to the next hotel."

Spark tucked the pillow under her head and tried to get comfortable. Impatience and worry beat through her, throbbing in time with her wrist.

Jennet hadn't messaged her back yet, and the taste of failure was bitter ash on her tongue. Some Feyguard she'd turned out to be. She dozed as the bus flashed through quiet towns and winter-bare fields.

Niteesh's hand on her shoulder roused her from fragmented dreaming.

"We're almost there," he said. "Hotel sweet hotel."

She sat up and rubbed her blurry eyes.

"Hey," she said. "Do you think you could talk Vonda into letting you have a FullD in your room, for extra practice?"

"So you can sneak onto the system?" Niteesh frowned and glanced at her wrist. "Seriously? You can't play, Sparky. What's the big hurry?"

"I have to try."

"If this is about the Terribles, I don't think you need to worry about them."

He glanced to the front of the bus, where it seemed Roc and Cora had been behaving themselves. Spark almost protested that the twins had nothing to do with her need to get back into Feyland. But they provided a good excuse.

"Help me, Nit. Please?"

He blew out a breath. "I'll ask," he said. "But no promises."

Aran woke after sleeping for hours. In the real world, he'd call it morning, but that word didn't belong in the Dark Realm's unchanging darkness. He pulled on his clothes, then grabbed his tablet. The dinosaur was a comforting lump in his jeans pocket, though he didn't plan on contacting the human realm today.

No, he was going to concentrate on that wall between the realms. Soon as he opened that, he could collect his reward from the queen and return to the real world a rich man.

And the first thing he planned to do was find Spark Jaxley. They had all kinds of unfinished business between them.

Without waiting for Thomas, Aran tucked his tablet under his arm and left the tent. He was pretty sure he could find his way back to the clearing Thomas had shown him yesterday. And since the queen wanted him to work on the wall, he figured the magic of the realm would help lead him there.

After one wrong turn that dead-ended in a marsh, Aran backtracked along the path and found the clearing. With a deep breath, he stepped into the mushroom ring. The wind rose around him, and he welcomed its familiar, sharp bite.

When the wind stopped buffeting him, he was even gladder to see he'd arrived at the mirror-image clearings. Slowly, he walked toward the middle clearing, one hand outstretched. He encountered the invisible wall and traced its slight curve until he felt the thin crack under his fingertips.

Time to see if he had the skills. Adrenaline rushed through him—half fear of failure, half excitement at the challenge.

He settled on the soft mosses of the clearing, the wall firmly at his back, and powered up his tablet. It flickered to life, showing the normal menu screen. Now—how to get the tablet to display the code, so that he could modify it?

After a frustrating half hour, Aran set his tablet down. Leaning forward, he rested his head against his bent knees. Nothing he tried worked. Not inputting search terms like "faerie realm computer code," or holding his tablet flat against the wall, or even wading through the guts of the tablet's operating system, hoping to find a new, hidden protocol.

Something was digging into his thigh. He shifted uncomfortably, then froze. Oh, he'd been an idiot. The dinosaur was the missing link. He knelt and pulled it out of his pocket. Holding his breath, he set the garish toy on top of the tablet.

The display emitted a bright flash, and for a horrible second Aran thought he'd burned it out. Then the light steadied, forming glowing lines of code marching across the screen. *Yes!*

Leaning over the tablet, Aran scrolled through, looking for something familiar—a chink he could slide through, a gap in the programming. At last, his vision blurry from staring at the screen, he found it.

Despite the excitement rushing through him, his fingers were steady as he typed out commands. The first two did nothing—just lay there, limp as dead worms. When he ran his third script, he felt the wall beside him shudder. Not only that, it became visible, the code revealed in glowing green rows.

That was the tactic, then: a subversion of the ENOX to PH converter on the back end. He could work with that. A tweak here, a nudge there, mapping to the underlying conversion and adding bigger parameters...

The wall shook again. Then, with a sound like a hundred china plates breaking, the crack widened a full two feet. Aran scrambled to his feet, then turned to admire his work.

The light from the middle clearing spilled through the passage, tangling with the shadows of the Dark Realm to create an intricate knotwork pattern. The air shimmered with magic, and promise.

The way to the mortal world was open.

CHAPTER EIGHTEEN

SPARK'S head throbbed in time to Bella Boingo's latest hit. The singer's voice reverberated through the stadium, and the thick, warm air barely felt breathable. Spark hoped the painkiller she'd taken kicked in soon, because her cue to go onstage was in twenty seconds.

The dancers hopped frenetically around the stage, and a synchronized light show flashed overhead while Bella sang. It was so loud, Spark only caught a few of the words—something about boys and candy and flying.

Bella ended the song and struck a pose, her mirrored costume throwing shards of light all over the stage, and the crowd roared. Really roared, like some hungry, devouring beast. Spark had experienced her fair share of adoration, but this was a whole new level of fame. Under Bella's bubbly-sweet exterior, she must be tough as rocks to handle that kind of adulation night after night.

"I have such an exciting surprise for you tonight!" Bella said into her mic, once the crowd quieted a little.

Spark's appearance wasn't really a surprise, but hey—she could go with it. She slipped her wrist splint off and set it on a nearby table, then picked up her mic. No need to let the world know about her injury.

"Help me welcome superstar gamer Spark Jaxley to the stage!"

The crowd went wild again as Spark strode forward into the blinding lights. She could just make out some members of the audience waving magenta light sticks in her honor, and the sight turned her smile more genuine.

She waved to the crowd, then turned her mic on and joined Bella.

"Thanks for sharing your stage with me tonight," Spark said. "It's a real pleasure to be here in Landover."

Bella put her hand on Spark's shoulder. "Thank you for emerging from the amazing world of Feyland to say hello. Speaking of which—we have some killer footage of Spark in-game. Check it out!"

The stage lights dimmed as the screens flared to life. Spark wasn't sure she liked the implication that she was actually a character inside a game, but whatever. VirtuMax and Bella's PR people had scripted the dialogue, and they generally knew what they were doing.

The audience screamed and applauded as highlights of Spark's SimCon demo played. Her defeat of the basilisk got a cheer that vibrated the bones of her skull.

The vid finished, and in the split second before the stage lights came up, everything went sideways.

A mournful wail cut through the air, loud enough to bring the crowd's cheers down to a low murmur. Spark's breath caught in her throat as an unwilling shiver raced over her skin. The call of the Wild Hunt! She looked wildly around for a weapon. The nearest thing was a backup singer's mic stand.

Spark ripped the mic off the stand, handed it to the startled singer, then took up a position next to Bella. Despite the hot twinges of pain in her wrist, Spark hefted the stand, holding it crosswise like a staff.

The air in the center of the stadium roiled, forming an unearthly ball of light. It hung, suspended in the middle of the vast space. Then red-eyed hounds emerged from the sickly glow. Baying, they lunged forward through the thin air, heading straight for the stage. Behind them, mounted on horses with flaming hooves, came the rest of the hunt: elfin lords and fey creatures, their terrible beauty almost too much for mortal eyes. And towering above them all, the antlers of the huntsman. Spark gulped in a breath of sweaty air.

Thing had just gotten very, very serious.

"What's going on?" Bella asked, keeping her mic off. "Is this some kind of VirtuMax special effect?"

"Get ready to fight," Spark said. There wasn't time to explain.

The first hound reached the stage. Spark swung at it, using the heavy base of the mic stand for momentum. She connected, and the hound went flying. Beside her, Bella kicked out, her high-heeled boots surprisingly effective.

The rest of the band got into the action as hounds swarmed the stage. The musicians and dancers were laughing and shouting, bashing away with mic stands. They had no idea it wasn't a VirtuMax special effects show, but something far more dangerous.

Floating in midair, the huntsman watched from the center of the stadium, his eyes black pools. He raised his ivory horn to his lips and blew a sharp blast. The hounds turned and ran back to their master, and the audience went into a frenzy of clapping and cheering. Damn—they all thought it was part of the performance.

Spark's breath came in quick bursts, and she set down the heavy stand. The fingers of her left hand were numb, and she hoped she hadn't damaged herself beyond repair.

The huntsman gestured, and this time the riders of the hunt galloped across the air. Instead of targeting the stage, they began to fan out over the audience, pale hands outstretched. Fear spiked through her. They were looking for humans to harvest and take back into the realm. There was no way she could stop them, not by herself.

"No!" Spark yelled. "Elder Fey, help!"

A thunderclap shook the dome, and the Wild Hunt halted, some mere inches from their intended victims. From the darkness at the roof of the stadium, a dim form took shape. Winged and ancient, outlined in eerie purple light, the creature spoke.

Cease, it said—though it was more like a voice sounding through her bones than any word said aloud.

"Our prey," the huntsman said, his voice the shadows of deep night.

No. Begone. The Elder Fey clapped its wings together, sending a blast of wind screaming through the stadium.

Spark closed her eyes against that fierce gust. When she opened them again, the Wild Hunt was gone—the last hound leaping through the portal. The glowing ball of light shrank to a pinpoint, then winked out.

The audience went mad—jumping to their feet and shouting until the stage vibrated. Beneath that surge of sound, the creature spoke to Spark.

The way between this world and the realm is open, Feyguard. You must close it. As suddenly as it had appeared, the Elder Fey was gone.

Somebody at the light board was quick-witted enough to bring up the flashing stage lights. Bella's drummer laid down a beat, and her rhythm guitar player started strumming along.

"Nice show," the singer said to Spark. "VirtuMax has some prime special effects."

"Yeah." Spark hung on to the mic stand, suddenly dizzy.

"Thanks for coming," Bella said, then flicked her mic back on. "Let's give Spark and the whole VirtuMax crew a Bella Boingo wave!"

The singer lifted her arms high overhead, then brought them down. Most of the stadium followed her action, the glow sticks and illuminated messagers flashing in a river of light.

Spark waved goodbye, careful not to move her left arm. Keeping her head high, she strode off the stage as Bella segued into the next song on her set list.

For all everyone knew, VirtuMax had just put on an incredible holographic show. Spark swayed, lightheaded and sick. She had to get that gateway closed.

"You did what?" Thomas shouted—actually shouted—and jumped up from the table, spilling his cup of tea.

Aran took a step back toward the tent door.

"I reverse-hacked the wall between the realm and the human world. Just like the queen asked me to. Now, will you come with me or should I go talk to her by myself?"

Even though he'd been successful, the Dark Queen scared Aran. He'd rather have someone else along when he went to demand his reward. Although Thomas wasn't exactly being supportive.

The bard's eyes flashed with anger and he clenched his fingers into fists, then uncurled them, over and over.

"You stupid, stupid boy. The mortal world is completely unprepared for the havoc the fey folk will wreak. Oh, had I but known—"

"What, you would have disobeyed your ruler? I doubt it. Look, the queen said that without access to humans, the realm would die. I couldn't let that happen."

Aran tried to ignore the sick clench in his gut at Thomas's reaction.

"Did you not see the crack in the wall?" Thomas set a fist to his forehead. "I should have spoken sooner, but I never dreamed you would succeed in such folly—or that Spark would fail to remove you from the realm. There is still time to undo the damage. Repair the break, BlackWing."

"It can't be that bad."

He couldn't close the gateway back up. For one thing, he needed the money and had won it fairly, and for the other, he didn't want to contemplate what the queen would do to him if he backtracked and denied her.

"You must close it." Thomas's voice was strained. "The queen and her court are dangerous. If allowed to enter the mortal realm unchecked, they will cause utter mayhem."

"According to you, they already have access. And there's a police force at the ready, right? The Feyguard can handle it. Now, I'm going to collect my reward, before the queen changes her mind."

He was beyond ready to get out of the Dark Realm and its treacherous loyalties.

On the way out, he grabbed his black cloak from its peg beside the door. He wasn't changing into court finery, but it wouldn't hurt to wear the cloak over his jeans and T-shirt. Plus it had a wide inner pocket big enough to carry his tablet.

"I will accompany you," Thomas said, his voice cold.

The bard's stride was stiff with reproach as he accompanied Aran to the clearing of the Dark Court. Still, Aran would far prefer to have the bard angry at him than the Dark Queen. Thomas wanted him to renege on his deal, but no way did the bard have enough power to protect Aran from the queen.

The purple bonfire flared up as they passed, and the noise of the feasting revelers seemed louder than usual. Harsh and chiming laughter filled the air, underscored by the sound of a furious reel played on fiddle and drum.

The queen reclined upon her throne, her face lit with a terrible mirth.

"Well done, mortal," she cried, beckoning to Aran with her sharp-nailed fingers. "You have saved my realm."

"Your majesty." Aran performed his court bow, complete with the cloak swirl at the end.

Half of him was proud, but the other half wondered if he'd

made a mistake. Thomas's reaction pointed to the second. Aran swallowed. He'd get his treasure and duck out of there. Whatever other issues were going on were the Dark Court's to deal with.

"Come closer," the queen said.

He took a step toward the throne.

"Closer," she said again.

Heart racing, Aran walked the three steps to the foot of the throne. The Dark Queen reached one hand and gently ran her nails down his cheek. Her eyes were full of endless midnight.

"Such a pretty one," she said. "A pity I have to let you go."

"Yeah. You do have to let me go. And pay me." Aran forced the words out, trying to keep himself from falling into the queen's fathomless eyes.

She laughed, the sound like ice shattering on a frozen lake.

"Ladyslipper, bring his reward," she said.

One of the pale faerie maidens left her place beside the throne. She carried a black velvet sack in her hands, and wordlessly offered it to Aran.

He took it, surprised at its weight. Anticipation firing his fingers, he wrenched open the mouth of the sack, and saw the glint of gold inside. Oh yeah. He was going to be set.

"Many thanks, my lady," he said, bowing again to the queen. "It was a pleasure working for you."

"The pleasure was entirely ours, mortal," she said, her expression filled with secret amusement. "I presume you wish to return to your world now?"

"Wait." Thomas stepped forward. "BlackWing must remain in the realm. What if something goes awry with the gateway?

The look the Dark Queen gave her bard made Aran shiver.

"Methinks there is more danger of that should the boy stay," she said, her voice treacherously soft. "The gateway is precisely as it needs to be, and you will meddle no more, Bard Thomas."

Thomas hung his head, weary defeat in the stoop of his shoulders.

"I'm ready to go home," Aran said.

The bard glanced up at his words. "Safely home," he said.

"Right." Aran said. "I'd like to be *safely* returned to my world."

The queen's mouth twitched with displeasure, and he wondered what fate Thomas had just helped him avoid. He tried to catch the bard's eye in thanks, but Thomas refused to look at him. Fine. It wasn't as if they'd become fast friends or anything.

"Fare thee well, BlackWing," the Dark Queen said.

"I'm counting on it," he said, hefting the sack and hearing the satisfying clink of coins.

The queen lifted her hands and frigid blue light streamed from her palms. She gestured, and the light enveloped Aran. It swirled about him like a blizzard. He caught a few last glimpses of the Dark Court whirling past, and then doubled over in pain as an icy knife stabbed him in the gut.

He fell to his knees, gasping, one hand going to his stomach, the other clasped tight about his reward. Had she tried to kill him?

The cold light faded, leaving Aran in darkness. Where the hell was he? He rubbed his shirt, and didn't feel any blood or injury. Pain had been the queen's parting gift.

Slowly, he took a ragged breath and tasted a familiar,

musty scent on the back of his tongue. He fumbled in the cloak's pocket and pulled out his tablet. Flicked it on.

The screen light illuminated the lumpy couch in the Chowneys' garage, the scabby walls and stained concrete. Relief flared through him, and he sat back on his heels. He was back in the real world.

Right behind the relief came sheer, bone-numbing exhaustion. Aran nudged the gold-filled sack under the couch, then powered off his tablet, wrapped the cloak tightly around him, and barely made it horizontal before his eyes closed and he crashed into sleep.

———

The second she got back to the hotel from the concert, Spark hurried through the quiet halls and rapped on Niteesh's door. She figured he'd still be up, watching mindless vids. The late-night hush was punctuated by faint snores, and the hallway smelled like bleach and perfume, the same as a million other hotels. Even the carpeting was one of about five different variations—this one in gold and red.

Niteesh cracked the door, then opened it all the way when he saw who it was.

"Sparky! Come in."

She slipped inside and scanned his room, her stomach falling when she saw it was empty of a FullD system.

"No luck getting some extra sim time?" she asked.

"Vonda said we could sim tomorrow, since it's an off-duty day. I guess everybody's been asking to play more, so she's planning to take over one of the hotel's conference rooms and hook up a bunch of systems in the morning."

"Oh. Great."

That meant the only FullD systems around were locked in the VirtuMax trailer. Even if she could break in, she'd have to figure out a power source.

"Everything okay?" Niteesh peered at her, his dark eyes full of concern.

"Yeah. The concert was loud, and my wrist hurts."

Both true. And even if part of her wanted to take Niteesh into her confidence, she couldn't pull him into that kind of trouble.

"Then why are you here? Take some meds and get some sleep."

"Yes, Dr. Singh. Whatever you say."

Niteesh stuck his tongue out at her. "See you in the morning."

She ruffled his black curls—a move calculated to annoy and distract him. "Don't stay up too late, yourself."

He batted her hand away and pointed to the door.

"Okay, I'm going." Despite her bleak mood, Niteesh always managed to make her smile. "Night, you."

She waited in the hallway until she heard the lock slide home. Then, instead of heading to her room, she went out the hotel's back exit.

It was cold in the parking lot, the night illuminated by orange street lights. Spark shivered and looked up, but there was nothing unearthly in the sky—just city-lit clouds with streaks of darkness behind.

She circled the trailer housing the FullD systems, and yanked on the loading door's handle a few times.

"Everything all right?"

Spark spun around, heartbeat banging in her throat. "Burt! You scared me."

Her head of security frowned. "What's going on, Miss Jaxley? You meeting someone?"

"No." She gave him a weak smile. "I just... Well."

There really was no explanation.

Burt waited a few moments, then nodded to the hotel. "Best we go inside. It's late."

It was—far too late. And clearly she wasn't going to be able to get onto a sim system tonight. One of the other Feyguard would have to.

She hurried back to her room, said a terse good night to Burt, then powered on her messager. Her wrist zinged her with pain bolts every time she moved it. Gritting her teeth, she sat on her bed and sent messages to both Tam and Jennet.

One minute passed. Then five. Why couldn't she reach them?

A strange shadow passed in front of her window. Heart pounding, she went and peeked through the curtains, but nothing was there. Nothing she could see, anyway.

Swallowing back the sting of fear, she tried Jennet and Tam again, then keyed in a third number. Roy Lassiter's contact.

:Hi Roy, you awake?:

:Hey there, beautiful! Missing me?: He sent a wink icon.

She let out a sigh of relief. At least one of the Feyguard was reachable. She really hadn't wanted to call Jennet's dad in the

197

middle of the night, though she would have if nobody else had answered.

:There's a problem with Feyland,: she sent, *:and I don't have FullD access right now. The barrier between our world and the realm has been breached. Could you go in and check it out?:*

:Whoa.:

Roy went silent for a long moment. She could almost hear him mentally switching gears.

:Okay,: he sent, *:I'll head in-game now. Stand by.:*

:Be careful.:

:Don't worry. I'll be back soon.:

Spark chewed her thumbnail and tried not to imagine everything that could go wrong. So much already had.

Somehow, in that one demo session, Aran had been marked by the Dark Queen. Spark didn't know how he'd gotten back into Feyland, or what kind of promises the queen made him, but it was clear he'd done the worst thing imaginable. He'd reopened the gateway—the one she and the rest of the beta team had worked so hard to keep closed.

How had he done it? And why?

Dammit, she needed to get into Feyland and track him down. This time she'd knock him over the head and drag him back to the mortal world if he didn't come of his own free will.

Despite the anxiety pulsing through her, Spark yawned. It was getting late, and the pain meds were making her sleepy. She made herself stand up and walk. Keep the blood moving.

After what felt like years, her messenger pinged.

:Bad news,: Roy sent. *:You're right—the gate to the Dark Realm is wide open. It's the first thing you see after logging on.:*

:You couldn't close it?: Worry squeezed her lungs.

:Believe me, I tried, but there's no obvious way. Force and spells don't work.:

:Maybe it needs more than one person.: She wanted to scream with frustration.

:Have you tried any of the others?:

:Tam and Jennet aren't answering.:

:I could make a bad joke here, but I'm refraining.: Roy sent.

:Good.:

: Look, I'll get Zeg in-game with me. We'll see what we can do.:

:Message me when you get out. I don't care what time that is.:

:Will do. Sweet dreams.: Roy signed out.

She felt dizzy with exhaustion. Rubbing her eyes, she sat on the bed, just for a minute. She had to keep trying to reach the others. She had to figure out how to get Aran out. And she refused to think about what fey mischief could even now be creeping out into the world.

Spark shivered, wishing she could go back and change everything—starting with the day she'd met Aran.

CHAPTER NINETEEN

ARAN WOKE with a crick in his neck from sleeping awkwardly on the lumpy couch. Early morning light smudged the windows, and a strange feeling of contentment hummed through him. It took a minute to remember why.

Right—his treasure.

Smiling, he reached under the couch and fished around for the velvet bag. His smile faded as he pulled it out. It wasn't heavy, like it should be, and it rustled instead of clinking. Throat dry, he sat up and opened the bag. No gold coins winked up at him. There was nothing inside except handfuls of dry brown leaves.

Leaves! What the hell? He pawed through, hoping that somehow the coins were still there, hidden at the bottom. But they weren't.

Somebody had robbed him—snuck into the garage while he slept and stolen his gold. He sprang to his feet and checked the door. The deadbolt was still in place. Turning, he inspected the windows. Locked and intact.

Even though part of him insisted one of the Chowneys had done it, another part knew better. Who would painstakingly replace each coin with a dead leaf? Nobody. Nobody human, anyway.

Those damn faeries had stolen back his reward.

Aran paced the chilly cement floor. He couldn't just storm into the Dark Court and demand his coins. The queen would laugh at him, and maybe trap him there for real this time. Unless he had a bargaining point.

Fine. He'd close the wall back up, and if they wanted it open again they'd have to pay in real money. The non-disappearing kind.

But to put that plan into action, he needed to get on a FullD system.

Aran ran one hand through his hair. First thing was to talk to Bix. He glanced out the windows at the pearly sky. It would be good to see the sun again.

Quietly, he slipped out of the garage and snuck over to Bix's window. The pebble pile he'd made under the bushes was still there. Aran flicked one at his friend's window. The stone hit the glass with a little tink. Two more pebbles, and then Bix appeared, shoving the curtains aside. He slid the window up.

"Aran—you're back. Short trip, huh?"

"I'll explain later. Listen, do you have your FullD yet?"

Bix scrubbed a hand over his sleepy face. "It won't be delivered for another two days. Two days! That is so tweaked."

Aran folded his arms against the cold. So much for that plan. He could try to break into a gaming store—but that was too risky.

"I'm freezing my ass off here," Bix said. "See you in the garage in a few."

He closed the window, and Aran snuck back to the garage, his brain spinning. How could he get access to a live FullD system?

Spark.

She would help him; she had to. And if he remembered right, her tour brought her back near the city. He grabbed his tablet and found the site showing her itinerary. The VirtuMax tour was due to hit Readle, which was only a hundred miles away. What day was it, anyway? He scrolled up to check the date, then let the air out from between his teeth in a frustrated hiss. The tour wouldn't be in Readle until tomorrow.

The itinerary glowed up at him and Aran read it again, not skimming it this time. Last night Spark had made an appearance at Bella Boingo's concert in Landover.

He tapped his fingers on the screen, thinking. The concert hadn't started until nine. The VirtuMax tour had probably stayed the night there—and might even spend the day. He had to get to Landover. Ninety miles, in the opposite direction from Readle. If he was wrong, there wouldn't be time to backtrack.

Although... He brought up the lists of the top hotels in Landover. If he could reverse-hack a magic portal, cracking a hotel's guest list would be no problem.

The garage door opened, letting in a cold blast of air, and Aran set his tablet aside.

"Dude." Bix shut the door behind him and ambled over to the couch. "Where you been, anyway? And what's this?"

He picked up the velvet bag and pulled out a handful of leaves. A few drifted down to lie on the garage floor.

"That's stupidity," Aran said. "I can't explain now, but I have a huge favor to ask."

"Whatever you need." Bix stuffed the leaves back into the bag and sat down.

"Could I borrow your grav-cycle for a couple days? And some cash."

Bix blinked at him with sleepy eyes. Then he frowned. "If my parents found out—"

"Okay, not the bike." Aran knew that was asking too much. "But I need bus money to Landover."

"No," Bix said.

Aran's gut clenched. "I thought you—"

"You're not riding the bus all that way. Whatever's going on, I trust you. I'll figure out what to tell my parents. Hold on while I get the keys."

Swallowing past the sudden lump in his throat, Aran punched Bix lightly on the shoulder.

"I don't deserve friends like you," he said.

"Yeah, well, you'll have to settle for me anyway." Bix grinned. "Whatever adventure you're on, though, you gotta tell me all about it when you're done."

"I will." Aran put every ounce of truth behind his words.

Even if Bix wouldn't believe him.

CHAPTER TWENTY

ARGUING voices in the hall outside her door woke Spark. She blinked at the dim light struggling through the curtains, her brain fuzzy. Then memory of what happened last night crashed over her.

She lunged for her messager, heart sinking when she saw the blank screen.

Whoever was in the hall, they were getting louder. And they kept saying her name. Scooping her hair out of her face, she went to the door and looked out the peephole.

Disbelief flashed through her, cold, then hot. She undid the locks and flung her door open.

"Aran!" It *was* him.

"Miss Jaxley." Her security guard, Joe, had Aran by the arm. "Sorry to disturb you. I was just escorting Mr. Cole out. Burt instructed us he wasn't welcome."

"Wait," she said. "I want to talk to him."

"You do?" Joe's look of confusion was almost funny.

"Yes," she said.

"I told you so." Aran pulled free of Joe's grasp and tugged his leather jacket back into place. "Can I come in?"

Spark stepped back and held the door wider. She knew she looked terrible, with her sleep-tangled hair and slept-in clothes, but that didn't matter. When Joe started to follow Aran into her room, she held up her hand.

"Just him," she said.

"But Miss Jaxley—"

"He's safe. And you can check back in a half hour, okay? Aran and I need to talk. Alone."

"Burt's going to kill me," Joe said.

"Tell Burt I insisted. Since that's exactly what I'm doing. Bye." She shut the door in his face, then locked it.

Slowly, she turned. Yes, Aran really stood there, hands in his pockets. She wanted to hug him. She wanted to slap him. She wanted to shake him until his teeth rattled.

Instead she folded her arms, wincing as she jarred her wrist.

"Are you okay?" He was suddenly way too close, setting one gentle finger on her splint. "Is this... did you get injured in-game?"

"Yep. No thanks to you."

His eyes widened with horror. "Oh, crap. I am so sorry. I didn't know—"

"It's just sprained. Though, yes, if you get injured in the realm, it carries over to the real world." She brushed past him, going to one of the two chairs set at the far end of the room. "Tell me how you escaped the Dark Realm. And what happened to the gateway between the worlds."

"Ah." He looked down at the floor, then back to her. "I screwed up, and I need your help."

"*Now* you're asking for my help?" Anger flared through her, and she was wide awake. "After our little encounter in-game, why would you even think I'd lift a finger for you? You managed to get out of the realm. I'd say you're doing fine on your own."

He sat in the other chair and rested his forearms on his knees.

"Ever hear of gold coins turning to leaves?" he asked.

"Faerie gold. Dammit, Aran. What happened?"

He let out a long breath, his dark eyes haunted. "I thought I'd finally be set. Do what the queen asked, open the gateway, get my reward, and be done."

"And it never occurred to you that the gateway was closed for a reason?"

"I…" He shook his head. "I didn't think too hard about it. It was a puzzle to crack. That's all."

She stood, fury whipping through her. "Let me tell you then. Last night, at Bella Boingo's concert, the Wild Hunt materialized. In *our* world. Do you know what that means?"

He sucked in a breath. "Oh, hell. We have to close that gate."

"How could you be so stupid?" She shook her fist in his face, then whirled away.

She'd never wanted to actually attack someone, until now. Mastering her fury, she stalked the length of the room, then back. Aran watched her, his shoulders bent in what had better be remorse.

"We need to get into Feyland now and fix this," she said. "You can fix it, right?"

"Yeah. I think."

"Stay there." She pointed at him, then grabbed some fresh clothes and went into the bathroom. As soon as she was dressed and somewhat groomed, she messaged Vonda.

:Come to my room, please? It's urgent.:

:Be right there.:

Bless Vonda for not asking questions.

Spark emerged from the bathroom to see Aran still in his chair. He was turning the pink stone around between his fingers, the one he'd given her. The one that, despite herself, she put on the bedside table each night in order to feel a little less lonely.

She was still so mad at him she could spit.

"Give that back."

She didn't wait for him to hand the stone over, just snatched it from him and put it in her pocket.

"We're about to have a visitor," she said. "Keep your mouth shut, all right?"

"Got it."

At least he knew better than to push her with questions. Spark pulled the cover up over the rumpled sheets of her bed, then went to the door. Before Vonda could knock, Spark opened it and gestured her inside. Across the hall, Joe watched from the open door of his own room, but made no move to come in. Smart guy.

"Whoa." Vonda halted in the middle of the room. "What's he doing here?"

She cast a suspicious glance at the bed, then back at Aran, and Spark hurried to answer.

"He arrived a few minutes ago, that's all. We need to use a couple of the FullD systems, just the two of us. I can't explain —but trust me, it's important."

"What about your wrist?" Vonda set her hands on her hips. "This is not okay."

"I know. But we have to do it now. Please." Spark went up to her manager, hoping Vonda could read the truth in her eyes.

Vonda studied her face, then exhaled sharply through her nostrils. "I don't know what you've gotten into, but I can give you an hour. One hour, that's it."

"Thank you."

"I bet you haven't eaten breakfast."

"Not yet, but—"

"Whatever's going on, you need to eat. Raid the room's snack bar." Vonda held up her hand. "Don't argue. You're the only one who never touches it. Niteesh decimates his, and the Terabins always eat the most expensive stuff."

"Okay then."

Spark opened the hotel fridge and pulled out a couple of nut-packed candy bars and cans of soda. However Aran had gotten there, she'd bet he hadn't stopped for a hearty meal along the way.

"I'll let you into the conference room where we've set up the systems," Vonda said. "And I'll tell the others not to barge in. But when your time's up, we talk."

She glared at Aran, then swung back to Spark.

"Right," Spark said. She tossed a bar and a can of soda to Aran. "Let's go."

Aran silently followed Spark and her manager to the conference room with the FullD set-ups. On the way, he ate the candy bar and chugged the soda, grateful for the sugar rush clearing his head. It still wasn't enough to wash away the guilt.

This was going to be tricky, in more ways than one.

He had to fix the code without giving away the fact he'd been trying to hack Feyland all along, try to get Spark to forgive him, and—hardest of all—escape the wrath of the Dark Queen.

He geared up while Spark argued with Vonda about wearing an oversized gaming glove. They sorted it out, and soon Spark was ready. She gave him a sharp nod, and he logged in, sending his avatar into Feyland.

Golden light swirled around him, making his stomach churn. He clenched his teeth against the sensation, and a moment later his Saboteur materialized in a faerie-ringed clearing full of shadows.

Spark's Kitsune flickered into being beside him.

"Good," she said. "We're in the right place. I wasn't sure this would work."

"Meaning?"

"I've already fought through two of the game levels, so we're getting close to the Dark Court. This place," she swept her arm out, "has the right mushrooms, and it's night."

He looked up at the dark blue sky speckled with stars. "Night, but not midnight. No moon."

"Yet."

She cupped her hands, and a second later held a glowing ball of flame. It rose into the air to hover a few inches above her head, casting a reddish illumination over their surroundings.

"Now." She turned to face him, her expression stern. "What did you do to open the gateway, and can we fix it from here?"

He glanced around the clearing. The place was completely unfamiliar. No mirror images, no wall of code. At least, he didn't think so. He went forward a few paces, hand outstretched, stepping over the pale mushrooms to the path leading between dark trees. His questing fingers met no resistance.

"Can't do it from here," he said. "We need to get closer to the court."

"Great. Do you have any idea how dangerous that is?"

"Good thing you're with me." His weak smile faded under her narrow-eyed stare.

"Come on." She started down the path, the ball of flame bobbing overhead. "And don't do anything stupid. More stupid than you already have, that is."

"Wait." He caught up to her and took her arm. "I get it. I totally screwed up. Believe me, I feel like crap about it, and I'm trying to make amends here. So you can quit riding me."

She stared at him a minute, and then her gaze dropped to the leaf-strewn path beneath their feet.

"It's not just you I'm riding," she said. "I failed. If I'd pulled you out earlier, when I saw you in-game, none of this would have happened."

"I wouldn't have come. Stop it." He held up a hand as she started to speak again. "You were hurt, the hunt was on your trail, and I honestly don't think you had the time to fight me into submission and drag me back, one-handed, to the mortal world."

She pulled a breath in through her nose, then let it out. "Fine. We're not done with this, but for right now let's focus on closing that gateway."

The night forest rustled with strange noises as they continued along the path, and Spark's ball of fire made the trees loom ominously. Shadows flickered over the trunks, and Aran set his hand to his long-knife, senses on full alert.

"Halt!" A figure leaped onto the path, blocking their way. "You may not pass."

Firelight shone off his sword and the burnished bronze of his chest piece and helm. Aran drew his blade and called upon his skills as a Saboteur to melt into the darkness surrounding them. He stepped off the path, carefully setting his feet on the dark patches of loam and avoiding any telltale twigs. If Spark kept the guy distracted, Aran could sneak around for an unexpected killing strike.

"Stand aside," Spark said to the armored figure.

The attacker moved closer to her, and Aran drew his blade. No way was he going to stand by and let Spark get injured again in-game. He lifted his knife and lunged forward in a deadly strike.

CHAPTER TWENTY-ONE

"SPARK?" The warrior lowered his sword.

"Aran, stop!" Spark yelled.

Twisting, Aran managed to turn his attack away from the warrior's neck. The blade slid down his opponent's armored shoulder with a screech, and the warrior pivoted, swinging his sword at Aran's head.

He ducked and pulled his second blade, heartbeat pumping urgently.

"Both of you, stand down," Spark said, pushing between them. "You're not enemies."

"You sure about that?" Aran asked.

"Yes." She nudged him away from the warrior. "Aran, meet Roy."

The warrior pulled off his helmet, revealing ordinary human features, and studied Aran. Neither of them said hello.

After a moment, Roy sheathed his sword and turned to Spark. "I was wondering when you'd make it in-game."

"You've been here all night?" Spark asked. "You must be exhausted."

"I'm fine." Roy shrugged, but Aran was sure he was lying. "I said I'd message you when I got out. What, you think I forgot?"

Aran shot a glance at Spark. This guy had her private number? He shoved down the hot stab of jealousy. After all, he had no claim on her—in fact, had blown his chances pretty spectacularly. Even if she did keep the rock he'd given her on her nightstand.

"What's going on?" he asked.

She turned to him, her magenta hair extra red in the firelight.

"Put your knife away," she said. "Roy is one of the Feyguard. And he's been doing his job of protecting the border."

"Spark, I know why you're here," Roy said, then tipped his head at Aran. "But what about him?"

"Aran's going to help me close the gate," she said.

"He is?" Roy raised one eyebrow. "Should I be jealous?"

"No." Her voice was firm. "You should be logging off and getting some rest. We'll stand watch here until you get one of the other Feyguard in."

"Zeg was here until recently. I sent him to get some rest. I can handle this."

Aran snorted. Roy's voice held a ragged edge, and clearly the dude was trying to play tough to impress Spark.

"Watch it, pretty-boy," Roy said to him.

"Roy." Spark set a hand on his arm. "Please."

Roy's look of resolution softened at her touch, and Aran

couldn't blame him. He'd cave, too, if Spark looked at him that way.

"Okay," Roy said. "I'll gather the others and send them in. Be careful."

"Don't worry." Spark stood on tiptoes and kissed him on the cheek.

Not the lips. Aran filed that bit of information to ponder later.

"You better do everything you can to protect her." Roy gave Aran one last, narrow-eyed look, then strode away toward the clearing.

"Nice guy," Aran said, finally sheathing his blade. "Are all your friends so sweet? And what's with the super-secret Feyguard club?"

"What do you think?" The warmth that had infused Spark's voice left when Roy did. "Somebody has to make sure the human world is protected. No thanks to you."

"How many are in the club?"

"Not nearly enough." Her shoulders dipped.

"Like, a hundred?"

She shook her head. "Try seven."

"What? That seems… inadequate."

"It would be plenty, if not for your idiotic choice to fling the gateway wide open!"

"Shh." Aran held up his hand. "I heard something."

The underbrush crackled again, and he whirled, going into a fighting crouch. Two spots of brightness blinked at him, and an instant later, a familiar, tattered figure sprang onto the path.

"Puck!" Aran and Spark exclaimed at the same time.

Puck grinned at them. "I am come to offer aid."

Aran narrowed his eyes at the sprite. He didn't trust the little creature—not after the way he'd "helped" Aran previously.

"What did you have in mind?" Aran asked.

Puck ignored him, and floated up to hover before Spark.

"You bear an injury," he said to her. "I shall heal it, should you desire."

"That would be great." She held out her left arm.

The sprite set two of his long, spindly fingers on her wrist. Greenish light flared, and Spark let out a yelp. Aran took a step forward, ready to bat Puck out of the air.

"I'm all right," she said. "That feels much better."

Puck gave a sharp, satisfied nod. "You are mended, across all realms. But now, 'tis past time you mortals continued on your final quest. Go! I shall guard the way."

"I don't think so," Aran said.

Now that he knew how utterly serious this gap between the worlds was, he was committed to closing it—and making sure that nothing else slipped through in the meantime.

"We can trust Puck," Spark said. "Look, he fixed my wrist, and he's helped out before."

"Better if we wait for one of your Feyguard buddies to show up. What if Puck lets something get through? Don't you think having a faerie guarding the way sort of defeats the purpose?"

"We don't have time," she said. "Vonda only gave us an hour. We can't waste it hanging around here, especially when someone else is volunteering."

"Some*thing* else, you mean."

"The lady speaks truly," Puck said. "Even now, the Dark Court may be massing, ready to push into the human world. Quickly now." He gestured down the pathway.

"Come on." Spark grabbed Aran's arm and towed him into movement.

Grimly, he followed deeper into the dark forest, hoping they hadn't made a huge mistake by leaving the sprite in charge.

"What's this quest Puck mentioned?" he asked, once they'd gone some distance.

"An extended questline I'm on. If I'm right, we need to find a golden apple."

"Sounds mythic."

She shook her head, her bright hair shining in the firelight. "No gods and goddesses in the realm. Just the fey folk—who are probably older than human history."

The memory of the Dark Queen's timeless, beautiful face sent a shiver down his back. He'd bet Spark was right.

Ahead, a glimmer of light shone between the trees, and the scent of wood smoke twined through the air. They hurried along the path and came to another clearing. This one held a fire in its center, and beside the fire sat a hunched figure in a gray cloak.

Aran and Spark paused at the edge of the trees, and the figure lifted her head. Long white hair spilled from her hood and framed her wizened face.

"Who comes?" she asked in a voice as thin as cobwebs.

She turned her head, seeking, and Spark leaned close to his shoulder.

"She's blind," she whispered, her breath a feather against his ear.

"Ah!" The old woman's face fixed on them, her eyes blank sockets. "I hear you. Come to the fire, so my hands may learn your features."

"Is that a good idea?" Aran whispered back.

Spark pulled her bow out. With one smooth motion, she nocked an arrow to the string. "You go. I'll cover you. Ask her for a quest."

Great.

Slowly, he approached the fire. The woman kept her blind eyes turned to him. Just in case, he slipped one of his knives free of its sheath.

"Now, now," the old woman said. "No need for that. Put your blade away, young man."

"I thought you were blind." He halted and re-sheathed his dagger.

"Ha! My ears know what my eyes cannot see. Tell me, your companion, does she stand, weapon at the ready to defend you from such a fearsome creature as I am?" The woman cackled, shaking with laughter.

Aran glanced over his shoulder. Spark, arrow still nocked, nodded at him to keep going. When he reached the fire, the woman stilled and held out her gnarled hands.

"Let me see you," she said.

"How about you give us a quest." He didn't want to go any nearer the old woman and her eyeless face.

"Favor for favor," she said.

Gritting his teeth, he leaned forward, close enough for her

to reach up and touch his face. Her fingertips felt like moth wings against his skin.

"Aye," she said softly. "A tarnished hero, seeking redemption. It will be within your grasp, have you the courage to seize it."

"Okay." Aran pulled back. "My turn. Do you have a quest for us?"

"So impatient, the young." The woman shook her head, the firelight casting odd shadows across her face. "I could tell you more, of pasts and futures, should you linger."

"No time for that," Spark called.

"Sharp-eared, that one." The old woman beckoned to Spark. "I will read your face as well, girl."

"No, thanks. Hurry it up, Aran."

"Very well." The old woman pointed one twisted finger off to the right. "In yonder stream resides the creature who will lead you to what you seek—but she is a wary thing and must be coaxed forth with a hazel wand and a bright berry."

Aran waited, but the woman said nothing more.

"That's it?" he asked.

"It is enough."

"Thank y—"

"Never give the fey your gratitude," she said. "It will earn you more enmity than you could guess."

"Okay then."

Moved by some impulse, even knowing she couldn't see him, Aran put his foot back and dipped into the formal court bow. A smile crossed the old woman's face, and for a starlit moment her features were those of a beautiful young woman.

"Come on," Spark said, beckoning.

When he rejoined her, she gave him a look. "What was that? The bowing thing."

"Just something I picked up," he said. "Let's go."

The path curved around in the direction the old woman had indicated, although when they'd first stepped into the clearing, Aran could have sworn it went the other way. Soon they left the firelight behind and the night closed in around them. An owl hooted nearby, and the wind creaked the dry branches overhead.

"Does this really have to use the soundtrack from a lame horror vid?" Aran asked. "All we need to complete the effect is—"

"A monster," Spark said, her voice tight. "And there it is."

Something shambled in the darkness in front of them, then lurched forward, illuminated by Spark's fireball. It was a huge man, wrapped round with clanking chains and carrying a wickedly spiked mace. From his chain belt swung three severed heads, their dead eyes open and staring.

"Fee, fi, fo," he said, his voice a deep rumble. "Jack smells lovely flesh and blood. Come play, my pretties."

With a roar, he lifted his mace high overhead, then smacked it down hard on the path. The ground trembled, and Spark glanced at Aran, wide-eyed.

He shared her worry. This giant looked to be severe trouble.

CHAPTER TWENTY-TWO

PULLING HIS BLADES, Aran melted into the shadows. He ghosted silently to one side of the path. It would be foolish to meet their adversary head-on, but the giant's back was unprotected.

Faster than his bulk would suggest, the giant pivoted.

"I smell you!" he cried, then smashed his mace down, way too close to Aran.

He leaped clear, heart pounding. Okay, it wasn't going to be that easy.

An arrow zinged through the air—Spark, taking advantage of the giant's distraction to mount her own attack. Their enemy batted the arrow out of the air as if it were a crippled mosquito.

"Stings and pokes?" The giant laughed, showing huge, blackened teeth, and the heads hanging from his belt swung back and forth.

"How about this?" Spark said, holding her hand palm out toward their enemy.

She chanted a string of guttural syllables, and from her outstretched hand a wall of flame whooshed. It hit the giant and he yelled, beating at his rags as they caught fire.

Aran darted forward and sank both knives into the giant's thigh. The neck would have been ideal, but it was above reach. Still, maybe the blow would bring the giant down.

Their enemy yelled again and swung his mace in a low, vicious swipe. Aran caught hold of the giant's chain belt and pulled himself out of the way, grimacing as one of the severed heads brushed against him.

"Off me, pest!" the giant cried.

Too quickly—Aran really had to stop misjudging their enemy's speed—the giant's meaty hand lashed out and grabbed Aran by the shoulders. Damn. He twisted, bringing his blades around as his enemy lifted him high into the air.

Aran stabbed the giant's wrist, but that only enraged him more. With a snap of his arm, he flung Aran through the air.

Trees spun past his vision and Aran desperately tried to orient himself. A trunk loomed ahead of him, and he brought up one arm to shield his face. The impact was going to break him. Dimly, he heard Spark yelling the words of another spell.

Everything slowed down, the air growing thick as honey. Aran hit the tree, the collision softened, though still incredibly painful. He bounced off the rough trunk and fell to the piney forest floor.

He sat up, head spinning, and flexed his arms and legs. Impossibly, he wasn't injured. Spark's spell had saved him. But now she faced the giant alone. He sprang to his feet, blinking with sudden dizziness.

The giant lurched and swiped, trying to grab onto the

russet blur of Spark's fox form. She leapt nimbly back and forth, evading the swipes of his meaty fingers.

Until the giant caught her by the tail.

"Aha! Foxkin head for my collection."

"Spark!" Aran sprinted forward, ignoring the pain pulsing through him.

Her figure blurred, then solidified again in her human form. The giant still held her, however, her bright hair clenched between his massive fingers. With his other hand, he drew a thin, sharp blade.

"My best prize yet," he crowed. "The pretty, pretty hair."

Something glinted in Spark's hand. Her dagger—but it was useless against the giant. She wrenched around, but she didn't stab their enemy. Instead, she sliced at the top of her head.

Brilliant girl. She was cutting herself free. And the giant was now low enough that Aran could do some serious damage. Without slowing, he raced to the giant's knee, then vaulted up onto his arm and plunged his knives into their enemy's chest.

The giant swung his blade across Spark's neck, but she had shorn off enough of her hair to squirm free. The giant's slice did the rest, and he was left holding nothing but a fistful of magenta.

"Aargh!" he cried, then dropped the hair.

As Spark scrambled back, Aran stabbed the giant again. A moment later, one of her arrows whizzed through the air, hitting their enemy in the neck.

With a slow groan, the giant toppled.

Aran sprang free, knives at the ready. His breath rasped harshly through his throat, the sound nearly drowned out by the giant's death moans. Beside Aran, Spark nocked another arrow.

"I think we got him," she said, though her bow never wavered.

"Yeah. Good fighting."

Warily, Aran watched the giant until his eyes glazed over, lifeless. The hand holding the blade went slack, the weapon crashing uselessly to the blood-spattered soil.

They'd won. Instead of a victory rush, Aran only felt tired. He wiped the giant's blood off his knives, then sheathed them.

"I hear the stream," Spark said, stashing her bow away. "Over there."

She tipped her head, her chopped hair falling in ragged lines around her face. Together they stepped off the path into the dark woods. Aran glanced once more over his shoulder. The dim bulk of the giant lay unmoving.

The cheerful babble of water ahead lifted Aran's spirits. Spark was right about the stream. She probably was right most of the time. Which meant he should have gone with her, and left the realm when he had the chance.

Spark's fireball licked red and gold reflections from the surface of the stream. Moving to the edge, Aran peered into the water.

"Do you see anything?" she asked.

Mindful that something might leap out and grab him, he carefully leaned forward. A flick of movement caught his attention, a flash of silver beneath the far bank.

"Maybe," he said. "Can you bring your fireball closer?"

The flame floated to the center of the stream. Aran

squinted into the shadows under the water and kept very still. Another flash and flicker.

"Some fish in there," he said.

"Are you sure?"

He'd spent plenty of time fishing with his uncles, mostly off the piers, but in the shallows, too. He knew a fish when he saw one. Even if it was a faerie fish.

"It makes sense," he said, turning to face Spark. "A stick and a berry. But what can we use for the line?"

"What are you talking about?" She frowned at him.

"Fishing. I think we need to catch one of those fish."

He glanced around, studying the trees. Most of them were evergreens, though a short distance up the bank grew a leafy tree with long, thin branches. He didn't know if it was a hazel, but it was the best choice they had.

"You get the sticks," Spark said, "I'll look for berries."

She caught on fast. Aran nodded, biting his tongue on words of caution. As if he needed to warn the most prime simmer in the world about the dangers of a game.

A few minutes later they reconvened on the stream bank. Aran had two branches, stripped of their leaves. Spark carried a cluster of red berries, still attached to a sprig of leaves.

"Here." She handed him the berries, then started messing with the edge of her cloak.

"What are you doing?"

"We need string, right?"

She plucked at the heavy wool a moment more, then pulled her dagger from her boot and sliced at her cloak. Aran helped her unravel a length of dark green thread, pulling until it was about twenty feet long. They cut it from the cloak, then sliced it in half. Aran rolled the slender strand between his fingers. Would it be strong enough?

"Do we need hooks?" Spark asked as she assembled her fishing pole.

"I don't think so. The old woman didn't mention them. But if we do, I can make us a couple."

"You can?"

"Yeah, out of sharpened twigs."

"You know a fair bit about fishing."

"I used to fish with my mom's side of the family." Before his life took a sudden turn into grim.

He bent and sifted through the pine needles on the bank until he found a nice pointy one, then poked a hole in the berry with it. Squinting, he threaded the berry and tied a complicated knot at the end. Seeing his work, Spark did the same.

"So... we just throw the berry in?" She waved her makeshift pole at him. "Any extra tips?"

"We're trying for that deeper part where the bank's cut away. And cast upstream, so the bait drifts past. Wish we had a net."

Spark shrugged out of her cloak and laid it on the ground.

"It's already ripped," she said. "A little fish slime won't hurt it."

"Fish aren't that slimy. But yeah, we can bundle the fish up, keep it from flopping back into the stream."

Provided they caught one.

He and Spark cast, his throw landing farther upstream than hers. Quietly, they watched the berries bob along the surface. When his bait floated into the shadows, Aran leaned forward in concentration, but didn't get a bite. Not the next time, either. Or the time after that. After a while he lost count.

Spark sighed. "I don't think this is even—hey!"

Her berry plunged under the surface and her line went taut.

"Now what?" She turned a half-panicked gaze on him. "I've never done this before."

Aran tossed his pole on the bank and grabbed the cloak.

"Go downstream—quick." He eyed the tight curve of her stick. "Don't want to break your pole. That's it. Let the fish run a bit."

Spark hurried along the stream bank, Aran right behind her. He kept giving instructions—when to pull back, when to gather up the slack.

"Wind the extra line up on your pole, like that. Good. Do you see it?"

Spark paused to look into the water. "I do! It's just a little thing, isn't it? I hope it's the right one."

Following his directions, Spark pulled the fish inexorably up. Its struggles broke the water as it splashed and flailed, its scales flashing silver.

"Hold it fast," Aran said.

He spread the cloak between his arms and waded into the stream. Luckily they'd hit some shallows, and the water was only a little above his knees.

As if sensing his approach, the fish thrashed wildly.

"Oh no," Spark cried as the red berry popped out of its mouth.

Aran lunged, cloak outstretched. The berry swung back

and forth on the end of the string. And the slim silver trout fell into the folds of the cloak.

He whipped the edges together and splashed back to the bank. Spark took his elbow to help him out, and, squelching with each step, Aran moved several paces away from the stream. He could feel the fish wriggling desperately within the woolen confines.

"Now what?" Spark asked.

"It's getting heavy," Aran said. "I think it's growing."

"Stand back." Spark pulled out her bow and took a wary stance.

He laid the cloak down. Sure enough, whatever was under the fabric had grown bigger, and it was still thrashing. He backed up, hands going to his knives.

The cloak fell open, and he could only stare. It wasn't a fish. It wasn't even a monster.

It was a girl.

Her naked skin glimmered like moonlight. White blossoms were woven into her long, dark hair, and her eyes were wide with fear.

"Hey there," Spark said, taking a step forward.

In an instant, the girl was on her feet. She cast a wild glance about the forest and, before they could stop her, bolted into the shadows of the trees.

CHAPTER TWENTY-THREE

"Wait!" Aran cried. "We have to follow her."

The maiden's pale figure was quickly disappearing into the dark woods. He and Spark plunged through the underbrush, barely keeping the girl in sight. Only her glowing skin kept them from losing her completely.

Branches caught at Aran's arms and the scent of crushed bracken fern stung his nose. They got no closer to the girl, but fell no farther away, either. Above, the unfamiliar stars shone down, distant and impassive.

The forest ended. Ahead, the maiden scrambled up a sudden hill, the grasses silvered beneath the moon. She reached the top, her faintly glowing form framed for a moment against the night sky. Then she was gone.

"Hurry," Spark gasped, though she had fallen a few paces behind.

Aran reached back and grabbed her hand, pulling her with him to the top of the hill. Except it wasn't a hill, but a grassy mound. The midnight landscape spread out around them, with no sign of the fish maiden.

In the center of the hill grew a tree covered with starry blossoms. And one perfect, golden sun.

"Oh," Spark said. "The golden apple."

"Do you think it's safe to just pick?"

Belatedly, Aran let go of her hand and readied himself for combat.

"I think so. After all, we had to fight the giant, fish up the girl, and then pursue her. That's three."

He wasn't sure what she was talking about. Senses alert, he followed Spark to the base of the tree. She reached, but the apple hung too high, gleaming far above her hopeful fingertips.

"Boost me up," she said.

Aran cupped his hands and they managed to get her into the crook of the tree. Carefully, she edged out along one of the lower branches. He paced below, ready to catch her if she fell. White petals drifted down in the wake of her passage.

"Almost there," he called softly.

She was so close, the golden glow cast a soft light over her face and the ragged ends of her hair. Watching, Aran held his breath. She reached, and plucked the apple. It parted from the tree with a sweet, musical chime.

"Got it." She smiled down at him.

And fell, as a sudden, furious wind lashed the branches of the tree.

He caught her, breaking her fall as the two of them tumbled to the soft grass.

"We better go," he said, though part of him wanted nothing

more than to lie there with her, limbs tangled together, and count the unearthly stars.

Overhead, the trembling wail of the Wild Hunt echoed through the sky. Way to break the romantic mood. They scrambled to their feet.

"Over there." Spark caught his arm and pulled him toward the far end of the hill.

A small faerie ring shone, nearly hidden by the silvery grasses. Without a word, he and Spark leaped into the center. He didn't care where it went, as long as it took them away from the hunt.

The familiar, chilly wind rose about them, and he hunched his shoulders against the gusts. After two icy breaths, the wind subsided and the scene cleared to reveal their destination.

Aran couldn't hold back his whoop of triumph. They stood in the mirror-image clearing, and though he couldn't see the coded wall, he knew it was there.

"What is this place?" Spark asked, glancing across at the other two clearings.

"The barrier between the realms. Look."

He stepped forward, palm out, until he met the resistance of the wall. He gave it a slap, demonstrating its solidity. Spark followed him, her hand outstretched. When she reached the barrier, she glanced over at him.

"Fix it, and let's get out of here."

Crap. Aran looked down at his hands, then back up at her. His throat tightened with the taste of failure.

"I don't think I can. Last time I had my tablet with me—that's how I accessed the programming."

"There's no other way?"

He shook his head. Damn—why had he charged in without thinking?

Spark pressed her lips together, then held out her hand, palm up. The golden apple appeared, shimmering with light.

"How's that going to help?" Aran asked.

"In a previous quest, I got three wishes out of a copper apple. I used them to get the silver apple, but now that's disappeared for some reason."

"Maybe you can only have one apple at a time."

She frowned at the golden fruit. "Maybe. If you hadn't been with me, I would have needed the power of the silver apple to help defeat the giant and fish up that girl. But I didn't use it, so it disappeared when I got the golden one. I guess."

"How does it work?" He leaned forward and inspected the apple.

"Rub it, and tell it your wish." She held her palm out to him.

He picked up the golden fruit. It was warm to the touch, and heavier than he'd expected. Running his fingers over the rounded side, he concentrated.

"I need my tablet," he said.

Bright light flashed, and he stepped back, almost dropping the apple. It had split in half, brilliance streaming from inside. Then it snapped shut, and the air felt colder, the shadows creeping closer.

Spark bent and scooped up his tablet from where it had appeared on the green moss.

"Okay," she said. "Get to work."

"Um." Aran looked down at the apple again. "Three wishes,

right?"

"Don't do anything stupid," she said, her voice distrustful. "Maybe I should hold the apple now."

"No—it's just that I forgot something. The other thing I need to make this work."

"Well, try it without."

Before he could protest, she swapped, plucking the apple from his hand and giving him the tablet in return.

"Fine."

He powered on the tablet. As he'd feared, it showed the normal menu.

"It won't display the code," he said. "I can't tweak it if I can't see it."

Blowing an impatient breath out through her nose, Spark snatched the tablet and gave him the apple again.

Aran gently rubbed its smooth sides.

"The dragon toy, please," he said.

This time he was prepared for the burst of light. When it faded, Spark bent and picked up the bright orange toy.

"What is this?" She shook it in his face. "Don't tell me you wasted a wish on playing a practical joke?"

Her lack of trust hurt, but he supposed he deserved it.

"I'm serious," he said. "Give me back my tablet."

"You don't touch this apple again." She snatched it from him and vanished it back to wherever it had come from.

"I won't need to. Watch."

He brought the plastic dragon to the tablet. The instant it touched the screen the display flared, then reassembled to show lines of code. Aran's shoulders dropped with relief.

"All right," Spark said, which was close enough to an

apology.

"Keep watch," he said, folding his legs to sit cross-legged on the velvety moss.

He balanced the tablet on one knee, the plastic dragon standing like a sentinel at the head of the device. Flicking his fingers over the display, he scrolled rapidly through until he found the protocols he'd changed. It shouldn't take him long. Unravel this bit. Re-code that...

He was dimly aware of the shadows shifting, of the air growing colder, but he narrowed his eyes and focused all his concentration on the programming. Not only was he closing the gap he'd made, he was triple-encrypting the whole thing. No other hacker would be able to open the wall again. Ever.

"Done," he said.

The wall shuddered, then closed with a whoosh and thunderclap.

"You did it!" Spark hauled him to his feet, her grip warm and strong. "Let's get out of here. Hit the log out command."

Aran lifted his finger in the signal to exit the game. Nothing happened. He tried again.

Spark looked at him, her eyes wide and anxious.

"We're stuck in-game," she said, her voice tight. "This is bad."

"And about to get worse."

In those few seconds, night had fallen. The moon hung in the sky, a sharp sickle. Branches rustled, and he caught a glimpse of gossamer wings, of red caps and sharp teeth, of flickering purple flame. Faint music drifted on the breeze, and the air was icy.

The Dark Queen was coming.

CHAPTER TWENTY-FOUR

SPARK GRABBED HER BOW, her fingers chilled to the bone. Of course she and Aran couldn't just close up the gateway and go home—the Dark Queen would not allow it. The shadows in the forest gathered thickly, and Spark's heartbeat pounded in her ears.

She reviewed her spells. Whether to use each element at a time, or throw them all together at once depended on how the fight went. She was confident she could make that choice in the heat of battle.

What she wasn't confident of was the strength of two mortals going up against the most powerful being in the realm.

Figures gathered around the edges of the faerie ring, like spectators at a match. Squat goblins wearing hats the color of blood were joined by twiggy figures with long, oddly jointed limbs. Ethereal maidens stood shoulder to shoulder with shambling bog creatures. All of them focused on her and Aran, their eyes feral and avid.

A rustle went through the crowd, and Spark swallowed the lump of fear blocking her throat. Striding toward them was the forbidding figure of the Black Knight. She remembered him from her former battle against the queen. Encased in ebony armor, his helmet was drawn over his face, the eye slits revealing only more darkness within.

He stopped at the edge of the ring, but made no move to attack. Yet.

The Dark Queen glided into the clearing. Her dark hair framed a face pale as snow, with high cheeks and eyes like fathomless pools. Spark glimpsed the death of stars in those eyes, and tore her gaze away. The terrible beauty of the queen was enough to freeze Spark's senses.

Wait. She shook her head and blinked frost from her eyelashes. Stiffly, she looked at Aran. A thin layer of frost coated him, his cheeks shining with ice.

Anger flared through her, and she called up her wall of fire, blasting it forth from frigid fingers. The heat of it freed them from the frost's embrace and made the watching fey folk cry out, stumbling in their haste to avoid that sheet of flame.

The Black Knight held his shield in front of his queen, absorbing the fire as if it were a black hole, eating up the light.

"Unfair," Spark said.

The queen laughed, the sound like icy bells.

"Mortal girl," she said. "Do not speak to me of fairness when your companion has cheated us."

"Cheated you?" Aran scowled at the queen. "How about gold coins turning into leaves? I'd call that quite a scam."

"We upheld our end of the bargain," the queen said. "You received your reward. A pity that our coin takes a different form once transported from the realm. Yet you may not break the bargain we had."

"Oh, yes I can," Aran said. "And I have. The gateway is closed, and you can't make me open it again."

He lifted his tablet and, pivoting, smashed it against the invisible wall. The screen shattered, pieces of plas-metal and glass littering the moss. Spark glimpsed a bit of bright orange in the mess—the plastic dragon Aran had wished for.

The Dark Queen's eyes narrowed into glittering shards of diamond. A frigid wind whipped through the clearing, lashing the branches of the white-barked trees.

"Take them!" she cried, pointing at Spark and Aran with her long, sharp finger. "What mortal meddling has begun, mortal blood will make undone!"

The Black Knight drew his sword and strode forward, a gang of goblins at his feet. Spark nocked an arrow and fired, but the point slid uselessly off his black armor. Beside her, Aran flung throwing knives at their advancing enemies. A few of them hit, but not enough. Time for a bigger attack.

She conjured up a wave and sent it splashing over the goblins. They shrieked and flailed as most of them were washed away. The remaining few halted, dripping and wary. But the Black Knight kept coming.

Spark lifted her bow again and fired. The knight charged forward, knocking her arrow aside. She danced back, throwing up a wall of air to stop him. That armor was a beast to deal with. A shot right into the helmet was her best—and probably only—chance.

As the knight forced himself through her barrier, Spark darted to the side and nocked another arrow. She sighted down it, pulled back, and let the arrow fly. It was a good shot, fast and true. Halfway to the Black Knight the shaft dipped, suddenly encased in ice. It plummeted out of the sky to bury itself uselessly in the bright green moss.

Aran appeared from the shadows behind the knight, his blades at the ready. He stabbed, and the Black Knight let out a growl. Clearly one of Aran's knives had connected. But now he had an enraged knight attacking him at close range. He ducked the swishing sword, then kept going, tucking himself into a roll that brought him past their adversary. Aran rose beside her, knives crossed warily.

The knight turned, and Spark smiled a grim smile. Aran had neatly manipulated him so that Spark had a clear shot at his helm.

She set another arrow to the string. As she released it, she summoned an earth spell. Two more arrows appeared alongside her first, made of wood and ore and fine fletching. The first one dipped, then fell out of the air, heavy with ice.

The second was incinerated by a glowing ball of magic.

The third arrow wobbled, off center, and struck the Black Knight in the neck. He roared, then charged them, fast as black lightning.

Spark threw up her hands, but she had no more spells to summon. Aran faded back—too slow, too slow. With sick horror, Spark watched the knight's enormous blade swing, slicing right for Aran's middle.

"No!" she cried, leaping.

She hit the knight's armored side, and it was cold and hard, like flinging her body against black ice. Aran let out a cry of pain and doubled over, dropping his knives. He clutched his side, then took one hand away. It was red and slick with blood.

"Sorry, Spark," he gasped.

The queen laughed.

"Hold her," she commanded, brushing past Spark.

Three goblins leaped to do their queen's bidding. Their claws dug into Spark's arms and legs, and one of them gave her an ugly, sharp-toothed grin.

Her heartbeat banged through her, but she forced herself to breathe. To wait. She had a few more tricks, but the timing had to be just right. The queen was planning to... Spark squeezed her eyes shut, then made herself open them again. The queen would sacrifice Aran. If Spark remembered correctly, a few ritualistic things had to happen first.

An unearthly fire kindled in the center of the faerie ring. Its flames burned sapphire and azure and deepest indigo, casting eerie, writhing shadows against the trees. The queen smiled, fierce and terrible, then turned to Aran.

"Now, BlackWing, you will pay the price."

She reached into the midnight folds of her gown and drew out a long black thorn. Spark tensed.

Chanting harsh syllables, the queen passed her thorn above the blue flames. They leaped hungrily. Once. Twice. Thrice.

The Dark Queen whirled, lifting the black thorn high above Aran's heart. In that moment, Spark transformed, her limbs compacting and shrinking, her vision flattening, losing its color. Four-footed, she sprang out of the goblins' grasp.

Her teeth closed on the queen's arm, and the Dark Queen

shrieked—a sound born more of anger than of pain. Spark's mouth burned from the queen's blood. She couldn't hold on...

She fell, back in human form, to sprawl beside Aran on the moss.

"The apple," he hissed, face taut with pain.

Spark conjured it and brushed her fingers over the top.

"Help us," she whispered. There was no time for specifics.

The apple split and flared, then disappeared. She looked up, and gasped as the Black Knight's sword cleaved down upon her.

"Spark!"

With a cry of pain, Aran heaved himself up and threw himself into the path of danger, covering her body with his own. She felt the sickening thud of impact as the knight's blow connected. Aran stiffened and cried out again. Then, slowly, his head dropped to her shoulder, his whole body going limp. She could feel the wetness of his blood seeping into her vest.

"No!" Spark's voice broke on the word. It couldn't end like this.

"Forgive me, my queen, for robbing you of your sacrifice," the Black Knight said.

"Fear not." The queen ran her long pale fingers along the length of her thorn. "There is another."

The queen gave Spark a look that turned her blood to pure ice. Aran lay unmoving across her, pinning her to the ground. They'd failed. Hot tears ran from the corners of her eyes.

They were both going to die there, in the Realm of Faerie, all their dreams undone.

CHAPTER TWENTY-FIVE

Moving like the wind over dark water, the queen knelt beside Spark.

"Farewell, mortal girl," she said, raising her black thorn.

Spark braced herself for the queen's strike. She'd rather die knowing it was coming.

"STOP!"

Five figures sprang from the air in the middle of the clearing. In the lead was a silver-armored knight, followed by a blue-robed mage girl, a bearded healing priest, a black-clad martial artist, and a mercenary wearing a bronze breastplate.

With a hiss of anger, the Dark Queen brought the thorn down towards Spark's chest. The knight sprinted forward, deflecting the blow, while the mage and healer hauled Spark and Aran away from the Dark Queen.

Tears of hope blurred Spark's vision. The rest of the Feyguard had arrived just in time.

"Glad to see you guys," she said. "Aran's hurt."

"On it," Zeg said, green light pouring from his fingertips to

Aran's wound. "You two get in there. Jennet, your dad needs a hand."

Jennet helped Spark scramble up, then sent a bolt of power across the clearing, hitting the goblin that was sparring with Mr. Carter.

Metal clanged as Roy and the Black Knight circled one another, Roy's bronze armor a brilliant foil for the knight's darkness.

In the center of the clearing, Tam faced off against the queen, dodging her magical attacks but unable to get close enough to land a strike with his sword.

"Flame her," Jennet said, raising her mage staff.

Spark called up her wall of fire, relieved to see that her spells had recharged, and the two of them sent their dual blasts toward the queen.

Flames engulfed her, and Tam danced back, lifting his shield. The fire reflected from its polished surface, bright orange. The queen laughed, then turned insubstantial as smoke, her black dress swirling about her.

Tam yelled and sliced his sword through that wisp of blackness. His only reward was more laughter, cold as frost.

At the edge of the clearing, a gang of goblins advanced on Zeg and Aran. Spark let out a relieved breath when she saw Aran was sitting up, his eyes open. Jennet's dad joined them, and he and Zeg began dispatching the redcaps.

A clang of sword hitting armor brought her attention back to Roy's battle. The Black Knight was pressing Roy hard. She needed some distance, and a clearer sightline to get a good shot. She needed...

Yes. The grav-board was still in her game inventory. Spark summoned it and leaped onto the deck. With a faint whine, the board lifted. She whipped out her bow and nocked an arrow, sighting down it to the knight's black helm. This time, she was making that shot—especially while Tam and Jennet kept the queen distracted.

Aim. Pull. Release.

It was a flawless shot—until Roy leaped into the arrow's path.

"Roy, duck!" she yelled, her lungs squeezing with sick fear.

He did, throwing himself flat without a moment's hesitation. Thank God. The knight looked up, and the arrow flew perfectly through the eye slit.

The knight let out an immense bellow and fell to his knees. He shook, and the clearing shuddered with him, the trees creaking as a rain of silver leaves stormed down. Slowly, he toppled, his black armor dull against the brilliant green mosses.

"Curse you, mortals!" the queen cried, re-materializing in the center of the clearing.

Her expression terrible with wrath, she passed one hand over her wounded knight, blue power flowing in its wake. He disappeared. With that, the rest of the fey folk fled until only the Dark Queen was left.

"You shall pay for this day," she said, her voice harder than diamonds.

She narrowed her eyes, sweeping her gaze over the Feyguard, and Spark shivered at the fury in those depths.

Then she was gone, and the humans were alone in the clearing, ankle deep in a silver wash of fallen leaves.

Almost alone. One member of the court remained, his

form almost insubstantial among the trees. The edge of night retreated, the stars fading into pearly twilight.

"Thomas!" Jennet cried, dashing to the ghostly figure. "I didn't know you were in the battle."

He enfolded her in an embrace, then let go. "I could not aid you, but neither could I fight beside the court. My part is to observe, and to scribe the songs and sagas of what has befallen upon this day. Bitter and sweet as it may be."

"Hey," Aran said, stepping forward. "I owe you—"

Thomas held up his hand. "There is no debt between us, BlackWing. I should have spoken far earlier, and bear equal blame for what occurred. My only defense is that I am beginning to forget the fiery passions that move the human heart."

The sorrow in his voice made Spark swallow in sympathy.

"Please, come back with us," Jennet said, her voice nearly breaking. "Surely there's some way."

"Jen." Her dad moved to stand beside her, putting his arm around her shoulders. "We've been through this before. We have to let him go."

Thomas sighed, like an autumn wind bearing the last fallen leaf. "My love for you both remains, in all worlds. But I must depart. Farewell, Feyguard."

He lifted his hand, his form already fading until there was nothing but pale-barked trees where he'd been standing.

For a moment, they all looked at one another. They'd won, though it didn't quite feel like a victory.

"You were supposed to get some rest," Spark said to Roy. Still, she was glad he hadn't listened. It had taken all of them to beat back the Dark Queen.

"Did you see Puck as you all came in?" Aran asked.

"No," Tam said, glancing at him. "I take it you're the one Spark came to rescue."

"Yeah." Aran grimaced. "I owe you guys my thanks—and an apology. This was my fault."

Roy crossed his arms. "So, what's stopping you from opening the gateway again? Or telling somebody else how to do it?"

"A lot of things." Aran looked at Spark, then away. "I don't need to be convinced that the Dark Court entering our world means serious trouble. Also, I triple-encrypted the code. Nobody else could hack that."

"Are you certain?" Mr. Carter stepped forward, studying Aran.

"Yeah." Aran winced, fingers going to his stomach.

"Zeg, I thought you healed him," Spark said.

"His injury was pretty bad. I poured all my healing power into him, and he barely pulled through."

Jennet set her hand on Spark's arm. "You should get him back into the real world. I assume you're simming together?"

"Yes."

"Can we trust him?" Tam asked, glancing at Aran.

Though he wanted to defend himself, Aran needed to hear Spark's opinion. He tried not to twitch with impatience as she chewed her lower lip.

"Yes," she finally said. "He tried to save me by sacrificing himself."

Jennet and Tam shared a look, and then Jennet smiled.

"That's good enough for me," she said.

"Fine," Tam said.

Roy frowned, but it looked like he was done arguing.

"All right, team," Mr. Carter said. "Good job. I hope we don't have to do it again soon."

"The gateway's back to normal," Tam said. "Which means we're back to regular guard duty."

"Whatever that is." Spark crossed her arms. "The Elder Fey are too cryptic."

"They have their own rules," Jennet said. "Our job is to keep people from stumbling into the realm, or get them out again if they do."

"Like that always works." Spark shot Aran a glance.

"I'm a special case," he said.

"I'd say." Roy's voice was dry.

"I'm late to work," Mr. Carter said, tilting his wrist, then shaking his head as he realized his avatar didn't have a watch.

"Me too," Zeg said. "Take care, everybody."

His character winked out, and Mr. Carter's followed. Roy gave Spark a last, regret-filled look, and was gone. Tam hugged her, then shook Aran's hand. Jennet did him one better, and gave hugs all around.

Then it was just Spark and Aran in the faerie ring. He bent forward, one arm held tightly across his middle.

"Come on," she said. "Let's get you taken care of."

And then they had some serious talking to do.

She lifted her finger in the command to log out, then held her breath. *Please, don't let us be trapped in the Dark Realm.* Thankfully, the air about her swirled, motes of golden light whirling until she was dizzy.

The clearing wavered and disappeared. The bright light faded, but still strobed oddly, and a high, screeching noise penetrated her gaming helmet.

Spark ripped off her helmet, then doubled over, coughing. The hotel conference room was filled with smoke. The fire alarm blared, lights flashing. She glanced around, heartbeat racing. It was too smoky to see where the fire was coming from.

"Aran!" she called.

She could barely make out his form through the haze, still sprawled in his sim chair. Fear pounded inside her skull—had Zeg's heals failed? She darted over and squeezed his shoulder.

"Wake up!"

She yanked up his blood-covered shirt, then sagged with relief. No gaping wounds, only a scar running across his ribs, a faint silver line against his dusky skin. He was still breathing.

Quickly, she stripped off his helmet and gloves and pulled him out of the chair. He was heavy, and she didn't get him down to the floor as gently as she would have liked. The air was better there, though smoke still scraped her lungs.

Staying low, she dashed to the door and wrenched the handle. It didn't budge. She tried again, throwing all her weight behind it. Panic pulsed, hot and frantic through her veins, keeping time with the blaring alarm.

"Help!" she cried. "Let us out!"

Spark pounded on the door, cursing the fact that there were no windows facing into the hall. But there were some on the other side of the room.

Coughing, she scrambled toward the windows, then stopped when she heard Aran groan.

"Spark? What's going on?" His voice was groggy.

She knelt beside him. "Fire, and we're trapped. Trying the

windows."

"Sec."

He sat up and stripped off his T-shirt, then ripped it in half. The cloth left streaks of blood on his hands. With a crooked smile, he handed her half his shirt, then tied the other section over his nose and mouth. Spark, trying not to be squeamish about the blood, did the same.

The two of them scrambled across the room. When they reached the windows, Aran stood. Spark took a few copper-flavored breaths, feeling dizzy. The smoke was starting to get to her.

He dropped back down, eyes bleak.

"Jammed," he said.

"Break it?"

There was a chair pushed into the corner by the window. Aran grabbed it by the legs and swung it hard against the glass. The chair bounced off, and he cursed.

"Legs first," she croaked.

He pointed the chair legs at the window and rammed it, his body shielded by the seat. The glass shivered, but held. The alarm shrilled out its useless cry.

"Damn reinforced glass." Aran dropped the chair, coughing.

"Get down here." She beckoned him to the floor.

Face taut, he went to his hands and knees.

"Any other ideas?" he asked.

Spark shook her head. She didn't even have her messager on her—it was on the nightstand upstairs.

"Hey." She covered his hand with hers. "I'm sorry none of this worked out for us."

247

"Don't give up yet."

"Lie down, anyway. Better air."

He dropped to his stomach, looking like a bandit with the blood-smeared cloth over half his face.

They lay there quietly, and Spark concentrated on breathing.

"There has to be another way out," she said.

Aran went up on his elbows. "We should check the whole room. I'll go right."

She nodded, saving her breath, then began crawling over the scratchy brown carpet. Smoke stung her eyes, and she was starting to feel lightheaded, but they couldn't give up.

Halfway down the wall, she found the air vent. She didn't have the breath to yell for Aran, so instead she kicked a table over. The clatter brought him running, though he was smart enough to stay doubled over.

"Vent," she gasped. They had nothing to pry it open with. Except...

Leaving Aran at the vent, she scrambled over to her sim system and grabbed the helmet. VirtuMax wouldn't like this, but it was a small price to pay. She set the helmet by Aran.

"Break," she said.

He understood right away, and gave the helmet a couple heavy stomps. They took turns yanking at the visor, until the plas-glass was loose on one side. Hands shaking, she tried to slip the edge behind the metal grill of the vent.

"Let me," Aran said. "Lie down."

She didn't argue, just concentrated on not coughing while he worked on loosening the grill edge.

A sharp whistle made her sit up. She glanced wildly

around.

"What?" Was she having an auditory hallucination.

"Scoot back," Aran said, taking her arm and pulling her away from the vent.

The grill flew off. A moment later, Niteesh stuck his head out.

"Nit!"

"Sparky! And random guy. Into the vent, quick." Niteesh held out his hand.

Spark took it and forced herself into the small space, grateful for Aran's boost. She crawled up behind Niteesh, and he moved forward.

The metal was cool under her hands, and the air was several degrees fresher. Still, they couldn't just stay there. The smoke would fill the vents soon enough.

"Aran?" she called, though it came out more like a croak.

"Here." He tapped her ankle.

She started crawling, following the waving beam of Niteesh's flashlight and trying not to imagine the metal walls closing in on her.

"Okay, slow down," Niteesh said. "Tricky turn here. But we're almost out."

The vent got darker as he slid around the corner. Spark crawled forward on her elbows. She could feel perspiration, damp on her forehead. The vent made a left turn and she tried to fold herself into its sharp angle. She wiggled a few more painful inches, then twisted. *Dammit, she was not getting stuck in here!*

Her hips cleared the turn and she slithered through with a gasp. She had no idea how Aran was going to manage.

Although he was lean, his shoulders were broad. She didn't voice any doubt, though, just went forward to give him room to get through.

"Hey!" She squinted and turned her face away as Niteesh shone the flashlight directly in her face.

"Sorry."

He tilted it up, then gave her a grin. He'd managed to pretzel his wiry little body around to face her.

"Nice rescue, huh?" he asked.

"Ask me again once we're out. Aran, you all right back there?"

He grunted. The vent creaked with the sound of buckling metal, and he swore.

"Aran?" She hated not being able to see what he was doing.

"Yeah. Just… a sec."

She laid her head down, the vent cold against her cheek. Sweet air filled her lungs.

"Nit—how'd you know to come find us?"

"The Terabins were acting sorely suspicious this morning, so I followed them. They were collecting stuff—a big trashcan from out back of the hotel. Armfuls of towels. When I saw the can of gas, I knew it was bad."

"Why didn't you tell Vonda?"

"I did—but not soon enough. The twins had already set the fire and locked you in. Firefighters hadn't come yet, so I figured it was up to me to get you out."

"Doesn't the hotel have a door override?"

He scowled. "The Terribles jammed it. C'mon, Spark, you know how simple most of the tech is in these places. Easy to hack."

Something about his words pinged her memory. She frowned, trying to chase it down, but the thought was gone.

"Thanks for coming to get us."

"Oh, sure. Anyway, Vonda's waiting at the end of this vent. If we can get there." Niteesh pointed his flashlight back at Aran. "Coming?"

"Okay." Aran sounded exhausted.

The metal screeched again, and he groaned in counterpoint. Then she heard him scramble up behind her, his breaths loud in the enclosed space.

"Go," he said, something ragged in his tone.

Niteesh turned, nimble as a ferret, and led the way. Ahead of them, she could see a square of light, coming closer. Closer.

Niteesh slid out, and then Spark wriggled free, falling into the waiting hands of the med techs.

"One more," Niteesh said. "Move back."

A moment later Aran tumbled onto the beige carpet of the hall. Spark sucked in her breath when she saw the fresh blood coating his naked back, then she bent over, coughing. Her lungs felt like they'd been scraped with sandpaper.

The closest med tech whipped off Spark's makeshift mask and stuck an oxygen supplier to her face.

"Easy there," the med said. "Slow, even breaths. There you go."

She wasn't the type to faint, but the blurriness at the edges of her vision spread, until the whole scene looked like one of those old-fashioned paintings made of nothing but smears of color. Someplace warm and full of light, with plenty of air, and no blood. Sighing, she tipped forward into that dream.

CHAPTER TWENTY-SIX

SPARK RANG the doorbell of the basic, middle-class house. Rain spattered the pavement and pattered softly on the porch roof. She glanced over her shoulder at the security guy behind her.

"Burt, I asked you to wait at the car."

"Just doing my job," he said, calm in the face of her irritation.

She turned her attention back to the door, willing someone to answer. A moment later it opened, and a sweet-faced woman blinked at her.

"Can I help you?" the woman asked. Clearly she didn't recognize who Spark was.

"Mrs. Chowney?" When the woman nodded confirmation, Spark continued. "Is your son, Bix, at home?"

Mrs. Chowney's eyes widened slightly. "Is he in some kind of trouble?"

"Not at all, ma'am," Burt said. "He's the lucky winner of an at-home visit from Spark Jaxley. Part of last month's gaming convention package."

"Oh!" She looked more closely at Spark. "You're the girl who plays those sim games. Please, come in, sit down."

Mrs. Chowney settled them in a beige living room with a surprisingly colorful carpet, then hurried off to fetch her son.

A minute later he hurried into the room, as gangly as Spark recalled from her glimpse of him at the VirtuMax party.

"No way!" He halted, staring at Spark. "I thought somebody was playing a joke on me. Are you really Spark Jaxley? Your hair's a lot shorter."

"It's a new look." She stood. "Sorry to bother you like this, but I'm trying to find someone. Your friend, Aran."

Burt had his home address, but when he'd called, Aran's family said he'd officially moved out two weeks earlier.

After their multiple ordeals, Spark had woken up in the hospital. Not alone—her mom and dad had been flown in, special delivery, but Aran had disappeared. No messager number, no note of farewell. Just out of her life like nothing had ever happened.

Except that too much had, and she refused to let him run away from any of it. At least, not without saying goodbye to her in person.

She had more than one reason to track him down, too. Not the least of which was the fact she owed him her life. And vice versa.

Bix's expression went wary and he slowly took a seat on one of the overstuffed chairs.

"What about Aran?"

ANTHEA SHARP

Burt cleared his throat. "It's nice of you to protect your friend, but we're not here to cause trouble."

"Burt, be quiet." Spark frowned at him. His tough security-guy manner was far from reassuring. "Bix, I met Aran at SimCon, and I'd like to get back in touch."

"Oh, damn." Bix slapped himself on the forehead. "It really was you at that party. I'm such an idiot."

"No worries. But… is he all right? Do you know where I can find him?"

Bix glanced at the doorway, then leaned forward. "He crashes in our old garage—but right now he's working."

"Working?" Burt's voice was laced with disbelief.

"Yeah, he's on night shift at the local Fry King. I think he's done at five in the morning, or something tweaked like that. Before the sun comes up, anyway."

Sunrise. Spark smiled.

"I know exactly where to find him," she said. "Thank you, Bix."

"No problem. Wait—before you go, could I get a picture with you?"

"Sure."

She let Bix droop one of his long arms around her, and smiled on cue when he pulled out his messager and snapped a selfie of them. He looked at it and pumped his fist.

"Sweet! And, uh, come by again, anytime."

"Thanks."

At the doorstep, Burt shook his hand, and when they got to the curb she waved, trying not to laugh at the moony expression on Bix's face. Another one down. Why was it the one guy she wanted to spend time with kept running away from her?

———

Aran scrambled down the path, letting the fresh sea wind blow the smell of fry grease off his clothes. At least his night-shift hours allowed him to come watch the sunrise most mornings, on his way back to the Chowneys' garage. Spring was finally coming, the air losing its bite, the green edges of new leaves showing.

The sky was already getting lighter over the water, a line of white on the horizon preceding the sunrise. He never wanted to take the sun rising for granted ever again.

Beach stones shifting under his feet, he was halfway to his usual log when he halted. Someone else perched there, huddled in a thick coat and looking out at the ocean.

For a moment he thought about turning around, leaving the beach to whoever had claimed it first. The figure shifted, and he caught his breath at the familiar curve of her cheek. His pulse gave a huge thump, then settled into a faster rhythm.

For almost a month he'd tried to convince himself it was for the best that he never see Spark Jaxley again. Clearly his heart didn't agree. He kept walking.

"Hi," he said when he got to the bleached log.

He didn't ask how she'd found his secret cove. The head of her security team was a pro.

Spark tilted her head and looked at him. "For a second there, I thought you were going to run away again."

"Hey." The truth of her words stung. "I had some things to do."

After the med techs had treated his scraped back and his smoke inhalation, he'd talked them out of admitting him to the hospital. He'd waited around long enough to make sure Spark was okay, and then ridden Bix's bike back to the city. The distance had seemed twice as far, every mile spooling out, cold and empty.

"You could have left a note," she said. "Or your number."

"Look." He shoved his hands in his pockets, then leaned against the side of the log. "I don't belong in your world."

He still had no idea what world he actually fit in.

Knowing where he didn't was a start, though. And accepting that his family would never knit back together, that his old life was gone forever. Things would never revert to normal in that house. Setch would always be the firstborn, the golden boy, perfect in his parent's eyes no matter how many dirty deals he did. Aran hanging on, hoping things would change, only prolonged the pain. For everyone.

He'd given up hacking, too. It felt right, but the grind of regular work was gruesome—especially the kind of job he could get with no references and a minimal background check. It was either midnight fast-food peon, or, even worse, waste disposal worker.

Spark looked at him a long moment. The breeze riffled the ends of her hair, which had been trimmed into an even line below her ears. It looked cute.

"Did you really think you could just walk away?" she asked. "After what we went through together?"

"I thought..." The words dried in his throat, and he swallowed. "It was the best thing, for everybody."

A weak part of him had wanted to stay, to whine and beg around Spark like a stray dog hoping for scraps. But he had too much pride for that, so he'd left. Better to try and make something out of the cloth of his own life, no matter how ragged.

"You thought wrong," she said. "You entered the realm, and battled the Dark Queen. That changes you. Don't deny it."

He dropped his gaze to the tide-slick stones at the water's edge. She was right. Strange things moved through his dreams, fears and visions he couldn't share with anyone. Unless they'd experienced the same thing.

"The queen said something, during that battle," Spark said. "It took me a few days to figure it out. You're BlackWing, the hacker."

"Not anymore." He hunched his shoulders, waiting for her scorn.

Instead she scooted over and put a hand on his arm.

"Nobody else could have done that—cracked the wall between the realms, then shut it again."

"I was stupid. Do you hate me for it?"

"Well, I don't admire some of your choices. But you fixed everything in the end—and you know your way around sim code." She reached into her pocket and pulled out an envelope. "This is for you, from Vonda."

"Your manager?" He took it and turned it back and forth in his hands.

"Open it."

ANTHEA SHARP

He glanced over at her. Her eyes were lit with suppressed emotion.

"Do you know what it says?" he asked.

"I have an idea—but believe me, I had nothing to do with this. Other than telling Vonda you were BlackWing."

Aran pulled in a breath, tangy with salt, and opened the envelope. Inside was a letter typed on official VirtuMax letterhead. Sometimes going old school with real paper was far more impressive than a digital message. More weighty and real.

He scanned the words, then backed up and read the whole thing slowly. Heart pumping with crazy hope, he looked at her.

"Is this serious?" he asked.

"Let me see."

He tilted the letter for her to read, then watched the smile blossom across her face.

"Oh, yes," she said. "VirtuMax needs to hire the best threat testers they can find. They need *you*, Aran."

"But my background—"

"The company wouldn't have allowed Vonda to make you that offer unless they'd checked you out thoroughly. The fact that your brother set you up is pretty clear, despite the crappy public defender that let the charges stick. And I think Burt might have given you a character reference."

Aran stared at her. "Your security guy? He hates me."

"No, he's just cautious and good at his job. Notice I'm alone out here?"

He glanced about the beach. No sign of a security team watching.

"I hope he's nearby," Aran said. "You're a little too valuable to be completely unguarded."

Spark rolled her eyes and shook her head at him. The pink in her hair was echoed by the wash of clouds overhead.

He refolded the letter and slipped it back into the envelope, his insides churning with choices. Of course, he knew that companies hired former hackers to help ensure that their programs and games were as impenetrable as possible. But he never thought he'd get an offer to trade his black hat in for a white one. Well, maybe gray.

Speaking of villains...

"I have a few questions," he said. "What about those two gamers, the Terabin twins?"

"Gone," Spark said. "All their daddy's money couldn't help them weasel out of the fact they deliberately set that fire. Not with Niteesh as an eyewitness. They might be able to hire good lawyers, but they're never working for VirtuMax again."

"They tried to kill you. And me." He curled his fingers into fists.

Her expression hardened, and she stared out over the water. Aran wanted to touch her face, stroke that grimness away.

"They'll pay for it," she said. "The trial's later this year. But I don't want to talk about them. I want to talk about you. About us."

She looked back at him, her eyes serious. Above them, the sky lightened to pale blue, and the sea shone like a broken mirror, bright copper at its edge.

"What do you think?" he asked. "Could you stand seeing me around?"

Her smile was answer enough.

"I talked with the others," she said. "You're invited to join the Feyguard. If you want."

"I do." It surprised him, how much that meant. And how much he wanted to. Despite everything, he'd found his tribe. And, just maybe, his heart.

"One more thing," he said.

"Oh?" There was a mischievous tilt to her lips.

Aran leaned forward and brushed his mouth over hers. He felt her smile widen, and then she yanked him against her. Their bodies met with a shock of rightness that reverberated down to his feet.

His heart thumped so loudly he was sure it would knock right out of his chest. He'd hoped, then second-guessed, then buried that hope way down deep, knowing he'd never see Spark again.

But she hadn't given up on him. Of course not. That girl was always right.

He wrapped his arms around her, kissing her with everything he was, and everything he hoped to be. Stronger. Kinder. Better.

She held him tightly, her lips warm and intoxicating against his, as the sun burst, brilliant gold, over the horizon.

EPILOGUE

THE GIRL HUDDLED AWAY from the cold bite of the wind, a crumbling brick wall at her back. She pulled the thin blanket about her, heart beating fast as a sparrow's. Already she had learned two things: the mortal world was a dangerous place, and she had just enough magic to slip carefully through its currents, provided she remained alert and wary.

Why had Puck let her through into *this* place?

Darkness had changed to light, then back to dark, a double handful of times. She'd learned how to scavenge for food, how to avoid the yellow-eyed men who stank of cloying smoke, and how to move, silent as a shadow, in and out of the dwelling places of humans.

As soon as full night fell, with its dark covering, she would make her way to the shelter she had found. There, she studied the world she had come into, learning from the flickering vids how to act and speak as a mortal girl.

The time was coming, soon and soon, when she must fully

enter the world of the humans and carry out the queen's bidding.

But not yet. Not quite yet.

Who is this mysterious girl? Find out in BREA'S TALE, a Feyland novella - or skip right to the next full-length novel, ROYAL: Feyland Book 5

THANKS!

Thank you for reading SPARK! If you enjoyed the story, please consider helping other readers find this book:

1. Lend it to a friend who you think might like it.

2. Leave a review on any site of your choice. Even a line or two makes a difference, and is greatly appreciated!

3. Sign up for Anthea's newsletter to receive a free story and never miss a new release!

ACKNOWLEDGEMENTS

Thank you to the many people who made this book better: the invaluable feedback of my first readers Chassily, Peggy, Matt, and my fine editor, Laurie Temple. Thanks also to Arran at Editing720 for quick, professional, and stellar proof-reading. And a great name.

For an absolutely gorgeous cover, huge thanks to Ravven. And for the inspiration to move forward, ongoing gratitude to all the indie authors and publishers who share their journeys and knowledge so generously.

I also greatly appreciate the readers who have taken the time to contact me, leave reviews, and give me reasons to keep writing. This series wouldn't be here without you! Thank you.

SPARK draws on a number of traditional resources, including my go-to books for Faerie lore: *An encyclopedia of fairies: Hobgoblins, brownies, bogies, and other supernatural creatures* by Katharine M. Briggs, and *Faeries* by Froud, Larkin, and Lee.

ACKNOWLEDGEMENTS

Readers will also find references to a variety of fairy tales and story archetypes, as well as the poem *The Song of the Wandering Aengus* by W.B. Yeats.

OTHER WORKS

COMETS & CORSETS

THE DARKWOOD CHRONICLES

Deep in the Darkwood, a magical doorway leads to the enchanted and dangerous land of the Dark Elves~

ELFHAME

HAWTHORNE

RAINE

HEART of the FOREST (novella)

WHITE AS FROST

BLACK AS NIGHT

RED AS FLAME

SHORT STORY COLLECTIONS

TALES OF FEYLAND & FAERIE

TALES OF MUSIC & MAGIC

THE FAERIE GIRL & OTHER TALES

THE PERFECT PERFUME & OTHER TALES

COFFEE & CHANGE

MERMAID SONG

ABOUT THE AUTHOR

Growing up, Anthea Sharp spent most of her summers raiding the library shelves and reading, especially fantasy. She now makes her home in the sunny Southern California, where she writes, plays the fiddle, and tries not to game *too* much. Visit her website at antheasharp.com, friend her on Facebook, and be the first to know about new releases and reader perks by subscribing to Anthea's new release newsletter, Sharp Tales, at www.subscribepage.com/AntheaSharp